THE IMITATION THIEVES

Books by Marc Lovell:
THE IMITATION THIEVES
THE GHOST OF MEGAN

THE IMITATION
THIEVES

MARC LOVELL

PUBLISHED FOR THE CRIME CLUB BY
DOUBLEDAY & COMPANY, INC.
GARDEN CITY, NEW YORK
1971

All of the characters in this book are fictitious, and any resemblance to actual persons, living or dead, is purely coincidental.

First Edition

Library of Congress Catalog Card Number 77–139043
Copyright © 1971 by Doubleday & Company, Inc.
All Rights Reserved
Printed in the United States of America

THE IMITATION THIEVES

ONE

Marlake sits on the edge of Lake Erie; sits uncomfortably, being on a headland which catches the first thrust of wind and wave; sits self-consciously, being a retirement, agricultural, and cottage industry town turned in recent years by a zealous chamber of commerce into a quasi-resort, a cut-rate vacation spot offering with an embarrassed pretense of interest all the brash and shrill pleasures that are expected by the tourist who has decided against the bigger, better resorts this year and who wants a good deal more to make up for the fact that everyone knows he has paid a little bit less.

Marlake is typical of small-town Canada: same post office, railroad depot, lawn-edged town hall, shady and quiet streets. There is a high school with a band which never wins prizes, two long-established hotels (tourism has added four more whose cheap appearance is a source of local moaning) and one each of the rivaling agencies a modern community would feel slighted without—Chrysler, A & P, Shell, Lutheran, Woolworth's. Suburbs creep thinningly away on gravel roads on three sides of town, are denied life on the fourth side, where Erie feeds its grayness on the road-width strip of beach, sand which was imported to cover the pebbles and has to be replenished every spring.

Marlake will never be an Atlantic City, nor now has it any desire to be. The chamber of commerce lost its drive when the revenue scraped in during the four-month season continued at the same undramatic level, easing merely one wrinkle from winter's frown, and there would be general rebelling were it not that the residents are able to reap

1

satisfaction by comparing their unexpectedly refined selves with the summer element.

One evening in early September the wind was gusting in from the lake to soar aloft bits of refuse, send newspapers into an eerie scurry across Lakeshore Drive, draw into a slant the strolling tourists and cause the Great Erik to keep one hand on his hat, which act made him feel disgruntled, knowing it to be undignified. He watched grimly, almost with determination, wanting his feelings justified, for hints of amusement in the eyes of strollers.

Erik was moving along the inner sidewalk of Lakeshore Drive, at a point where most of Marlake's impermanent entertainments had gathered together, as if by combining their noises and brassy lighting they hoped to show that the old favorites were every bit as good as the new. Midway rides and questionable exhibitions elbowed for face space with refreshment stands of smiling smells, side shows, ball games, and clutches of one-arm bandits, leaving the remainder of the three miles of local lakefront to the boardinghouses, motels, and weekend cottages that always looked desolate, even hated.

The Great Erik brought down the protective hand to look at his watch. At once his hat was jerked off by the wind. Stopping, throwing out both arms wildly, he managed with scrabbling fingers to catch his hat before it was flown away.

From a group of passing girls came giggles which might or might not have been directed at Erik. But he flushed at the thought that they might. Cramming the soft trilby into his topcoat pocket, straightening his five-feet-six-and-one-quarter inches, he strode stiffly on. He felt annoyed and satisfied.

Several people stopped to look back after Erik as he passed. They would frown: then nod with recognition and be pleased with themselves for having seen a celebrity. Later, in boardinghouse or beer parlor, they would perhaps casually drop, "Saw the Great Erik tonight on the front. Him what's at the Grand. I was this close."

Erik would have passed unnoticed and unrecognized were it not for the black patch he wore over his left eye. This it was that made people say to themselves, locally, "Ah, the Great Erik," and, generally, "What an interesting-looking man." Without the patch, even in the slimmest of crowds, he would have drawn only the most idle of attention.

Erik knew he was not a striking figure. Small, thin, quietly dressed, he was aware of being saved from insignificance only by the black patch. It gave him an air of distinction, a raffishness, a cosmopolitan look which in most cases kept people from seeing the smooth face, neat girlish mouth and nose, tepid chin and boyish hair style; kept them from noticing initially the nervous gestures and shyness. He looked younger than his thirty-three years, looked somewhat immature. Yet for all the innocuousness of his features, there lay deep in that pale-blue eye a cunning, an arrogance, a lack of humor, that made the acutely perceptive uneasy.

Erik came to the end of the row of amusements and drew to a stop at the mouth of Waterloo Street. A hundred yards along, the street's commercial property finished at a railroad crossing; beyond was strictly residential, neat houses set in lines as boringly straight as the core of a blue pencil.

Midway down Waterloo Street's business end, lurking dimly back from the mediocre front like the second cousin of a poor relation, was a dusty relic: a building of ornate design faced with glazed brown tile: a music hall, vaudeville theater. It made you think of some old woman, rusty with age, proudly thrusting to an indifferent world her every faded flounce and frill, locket and bangle.

Light bulbs spelled out G AND. The R had fused weeks before and no one was concerned enough to set it right. Why waste time and money? In less than a month the show would close and the theater would die; in its place would be born a bowling alley. The same question answered the forlorn washed-out posters which whispered

3

Modern Vaudeville
The Great Erik—Master of Illusion
The Harem Girls—Beauty Unveiled
Miranda—Fabulous Contortionist
Plus Other Top Line Acts.

Erik let his eye rest for a moment on the name of the fabulous contortionist before turning from the music hall, whose front was deserted, and looking lakeward at a replica of a paddle riverboat, permanently moored, which housed a theater. There, from the box office, grew a line of people wanting tickets for a show that was composed solely of hairy teen-age singers.

For the first time in days Erik forgot both Miranda and the plan. He sighed with jealousy. He was jealous not only of the boat show but of the Empire, where an American crooner held languorous sway, and of the Princess, where familiar faces from television played a smutty farce.

Sighing again he walked on along the lakeshore, not bothering to glance aside as was his wont at a billboard which bore a stained picture of himself, complete with top hat, white tie, and black patch.

It was too bad, he thought morosely, that such feebleness, such lack of talent, training and theatrical background should be drawing such eager crowds, when real artists, pros, were lucky to fill half the seats. It was unfair. His own training had been going on for years, starting in school in Vancouver, where he had become interested in sleight of hand and had caught the greasepaint fever by acting in school plays. After twelve months in Los Angeles, days working at a store which created and sold illusionist's equipment, evenings with a Little Theatre group, came years of practice, striving to perfect the art for which he had a definite gift and to create an original act that would show it off, subsidized the while by his mother, with the occasional perk from a performance in a private home, a women's club, a trade convention. Then followed two glorious years as assistant to a celebrated magician, touring the capitals of three continents, a happy time. After the great man's retirement came a period of stagnation, back to Mother and the odd gig. Eventually, the gigs grew more frequent, his fee increased, he got mentions in the papers and was offered a date by a TV station. An agent caught the act, took him on, booked him into British Columbia clubs for the winter, into theaters in every province for the next year and into Marlake's Grand as top of the bill for this summer. That was background. That was experience. Not jumped up overnight.

Erik quivered in a taut chin and squared his narrow shoulders.

Seconds later he relaxed sadly as it occurred to him that for all his training, the public remained apathetic, at least hereabouts. The Marlake season had accomplished nothing so far as furthering his career was concerned. Marlake was a dead end. There was nothing in sight now other than a couple of club dates and an offered tour of Australia.

Still, the Great Erik thought, the summer hadn't been too bad. And, of course, if it hadn't been for the Grand he would never have met Miranda, and fallen in love, nor would he have met the others and come within sight of wealth.

As his thoughts switched to the plan, Erik slowed. His youthful face tightened into looking its age. The bridge of his nose grew white. He was displaying strong emotion.

A glance at his watch told him he had an hour before he was due at the theater. He had known that already. What the watch really told him was that the time had come for a call at Mr. Mortimer's.

The smaller of Marlake's two poolrooms hung out above a chain store in Waterloo Street. Mortimer's Billiards Emporium, as respectable as money, had five tables side by side down the center of a long hall that smelled of dust and no daylight. The tables were pale with age, their ivories pock-marked with use. On the walls were racks of wavy cues, scoreboards with matchsticks for pegs, signs denying the instincts of swearers and spitters, a poster requesting old clothes for African missions, and a huge mirror which bore the brand name of a chocolate company that had been defunct for twenty years.

At one end of the room swing doors led to descending stone steps, the other held a counter which supported a showcase of sandwiches and a copper tea urn whose top leaked friendly eddies of steam.

Behind his counter now stood Mr. Mortimer, owner and manager, on duty every work day from eight-thirty until midnight. He dined here on his own sandwiches, which he sparingly cut each morning. The poolhall was his home; the cottage where he slept and spent long Sundays was to him as impersonal as the housing of a Gideon Bible. He had surrounded himself behind his counter with parlor whatnots, photographs of his parents and wife, long dead all, a stuffed fish, books and pictures, all of which gave the place the look of a child's game of house in the corner of a barn. Out of sight behind the counter was a chintz-covered chair where he napped.

It was naptime at the moment, being the late afternoon lull, all five tables sleeping and only one person in view, a pensioner making himself unnoticeable in a niche by the door.

Mr. Mortimer, however, was not napping. He was kept from his customary doziness by a thrilling thought. Money. *Moneymoneymoneymoney.*

His fingers drummed rapidly on the countertop.

Money was not Mr. Mortimer's god. His ambition was. But since this ambition could be realized only with money, money was treated with suitable reverence, the way a pilgrim would regard the road to Mecca or a dog the butcher's apron.

The thrill from his present thinking was new, recent. Usually his thoughts in this field lacked drama; but then, the sums he usually thought about lacked drama too.

Mr. Mortimer was a saver and scraper—a shaver of cheese to make an extra sandwich, a switcher-off of lights to save a fraction of a watt, an arguer over playing times to add another minute. He did his own shoe repairs and laundry.

6

He also would have done his own charring in the hall except that the effort would rouse his lumbago.

And yet Mr. Mortimer was no miser, no pointless hoarder of cash. While his fingers and brain counted, a higher plane of his mind was fixed firmly on his ambition, which until now, recently, had been too great and grand a concept to be examined in a mundane, planning sort of way. But now . . .

Moneymoneymoneymoney.

The thrill tickling up through his stomach, he turned quickly to the tea urn to escape his thoughts. After all, he told himself, it was probably just wishful thinking. The plan might never get anywhere.

Not until he had finished adding to his tea sugar and milk in measures which a chemist might have admired for their accuracy did his mind return to its excitement. He stirred the cup with dithery vigor.

Mr. Mortimer, at balding fifty, was tall and loosely made and stooping; he seemed to be held from falling forward by his feet, long and narrow, flat and splayed, clinging to the ground like slugs. His blue serge suit, as shiny as glee, was too short in the legs and all achoke in the sleeves. He wore white collars on striped shirts and his tie was the only one he owned.

He had a plump face with a snub nose, snub chin, prim little mouth, prim little mustache. Eyes being the snide betrayers of character that they are, except with born liars, his brown pupils abnegated the officious mustache by showing temerity, uncertainty, and innocence. Mr. Mortimer was a gentle man.

He was also a cautious man. Not cautious in the mere suspenders-with-a-belt way, but in the way that would make unmarried lovers employ male and female contraceptive pills, a condom, a diaphragm, and then put off intercourse until the moon was right. And if this super caution was beginning to stagger, Mr. Mortimer could hardly be blamed. Only the essence of love competes with the smell of money in seducing reason.

Moneymoneymon—

7

Again he forced away the thrilling thought.

Finished with his tea, he left his post and strolled down the hall, soft hands clasped behind to balance his lean but parting at times in order to pridefully touch a table or straighten a cue.

He nodded at the old man, who, showing the respect due to the king of Mortimer's Billiards Emporium, bobbed a bow and made an amorphous gesture which implied forelock-tugging.

Mr. Mortimer, who was known by that name to everyone, even to himself, stopped by the doors and looked above them at a clock. He wondered if the others would turn up tonight—and immediately felt that they would. Despite the impasse, the plan was irresistible. Just to talk about it gave pleasure. They would turn up all right.

The Kwik Kar Wash on the dwindling end of Main Street was a long tunnel of corrugated tin. Inside, the bedlam of scurrying washers, downpour of water and blasts of hot air made an uncomfortable mismatch with the ponderously creeping line of cars.

At the exit, Lefty Steel tiredly performed the job which suited him best, the one which taxed him the least in mind and body. He uncoupled the cars and flicked a leather at fugitive drops of water.

Lefty Steel was twenty-five. His features were vague, as if still in the formation stage, the nose a smooth protuberance like a tongue in a cheek, the whole unmarked by lines. There were pimples on his chin. His patternless hair was worn overlong in oil-fused hanks stretched back from his brow and fronting his ears were fuzzy attempts at sideburns.

When his mind was unoccupied, Lefty Steel's expression was cheerful; or, more exactly, his mouth smiled. It was a smile that charmed everyone and made them forget he was unprepossessing and spotty.

Smiling, Lefty worked on without a thought in his head. He was waiting for this fiction to be over and for reality to begin.

The waiting ended now when appeared a man who bore the same canceled stamp as Lefty Steel, one clearly stating that vaulting ambition o'erates itself.

The newcomer said, "Hi. How goes it?"

"So-so," said Lefty. He removed his rubber apron, tossed it with the wash leather to his evening replacement and strolled off. "See you tomorrow."

As he entered a dusk-dim alley, Lefty lost his tiredness. The steps he took might have been a thousand miles long, so far did they remove him from his job. He lit a cigarette, performing the rite with deliberate movements, like someone aware of being watched. The cigarette he lodged in an extreme corner of his mouth, the match he struck by flicking its sulphur with a thumb nail.

Where alley met street Lefty stopped. He did a curious thing. Moving his back close to the wall, flattening himself there, he looked with uptilted head out onto the street, which was spare of people.

He narrowed eyes now aglint with cunning and skipped them about to search every doorway, scrutinize every stroller. Part of his mind stood back to observe the intriguing shot of himself posed against the brickwork.

Assured of the street's safety, he took a deep drag on his cigarette before tossing it away, shuffled his shoulders, twisted his lips into a grimace of toughness and stepped out, walking with a swagger.

As far as Lefty Steel of the moment was concerned he was not a skinny young man, pale and pimply; he was a handsome, tanned tough guy with the lithe body of a boxer. Nor was he wearing shapeless slacks and an off-the-peg jacket that rode up at the back and hung a deep crease around his neck; he wore a snappy drape suit of the type affected yesteryear by American hoodlums who were following the mandates of Hollywood producers who had believed that such styles were affected by American hoodlums.

This seeing of himself as others did not stemmed from his first Chicago period, which had begun several years before with the showing on TV of old gangster films. While

9

sartorially he had remained constant, Lefty had been convinced, in turn, that he was the spitting image of Alan Ladd, Humphrey Bogart, Jimmy Cagney, George Raft, and Jack La Rue.

Nowadays, after a stretch of fleeting infidelities—superspies, private dicks, hunted war criminals—he was convinced due to the rise of Continental crime movies that he was the double of a French actor whose name he couldn't pronounce. But this too was passing. He was veering toward his first love now that television had started rerunning the reruns. His second Chicago period stood in wait.

There were disquieting times when he didn't know who he was or what, if he were a crook or an actor playing a crook or himself playing at acting. There were other confusions too. Mostly though, he knew he was a gangster on the run, pretending to be a carwasher. Or did the gangster only imagine that other life? Yes, it was quite confusing at times.

Also dating from the height of Chicago Period One was the name Lefty. He had been christened Ronald. It made him cringe. So to match the acceptable Steel he had chosen Lefty, and enforced it on the acquaintances made when he thankfully left school to start on a series of futureless jobs.

An incurable dramatic, Lefty's life of crime was pure imagination. He had never committed the smallest misdemeanor. In fact he was honest, twice having found wallets and given them to the authorities. He was, however, known to the police, for occasionally they would get a call about a prowler, and, investigating, find Lefty. Grinning, they would send him on his way. They thought him funny. They were wrong.

Lefty came out onto the lakefront and walked toward the central run of amusements. If any of the people passing threw him a glance he knew they would say to each other: "Wonder who he is," "Looks like a tough 'un," "Wouldn't care to meet him on a dark night." Or even, "A crook from Paris, you can see."

He turned into Waterloo Street. He slowed, his swagger

dying, forgotten, as his thoughts went to the plan which was trying to hatch itself in the poolroom.

It was so wonderful, so big, so like something out of Warner Brothers, that often when meeting the other men he was surprised to find them actually there, in the flesh, real.

He was in on a caper. He was one of a mob.

Lefty's eyebrows and lips began to dither his excitement. Stopping by the poolhall doorway he drew a deep breath. It would never do to show the others how thrilled he was. And his excitement made him a little embarrassed himself. He worked hard at achieving calmness.

When his face settled he lit a cigarette in his usual style, made a big thing of throwing away the match, treated Waterloo Street to a fierce scrutiny and slid hard-eyed into the doorway.

At the street's commercial limit, flush against the railroad fence, was a store whose one window displayed a doughnut machine.

Oliver Jet came out of the shop door. He glanced back and up, at the lighted window of the living quarters, wondering if he were wise in allowing Jonesy and Pel to spend so much time together. Such a simple thing could lead to trouble. It was the base ingredient of the eternal triangle.

But what, he thought, could he do? Lock Pel in her room whenever he went out? Forbid her to speak to Jonesy? Of course not.

He shrugged and set off up the street.

Oliver Jet was a man of middle age, middle height and build, middle degree of genteel seediness. His handsome features were turning to the thickness of advancing years. He had dark wavy hair a shade too long and held from graying other than at the temples by home applications of dye. Most notable were his eyes. Large and tender brown, they shone with compassion, sorrow, and love, the eyes of a Mother Superior or a backward child or a lame cocker spaniel.

A difficult person to place in category, was Oliver Jet.

The inordinately attractive eyes, the knowing mouth, the authoritative walk, the cultured accent, the well-cut suit with its baggy knees and touches of glue on its cuffs to hold straying threads, the polished, commanding manner, the cracked shoes and the carefully tended fingernails—these the observer found ambiguous.

Was he an actor, resting? A disbarred lawyer? A bankrupt? A black sheep? An aging ladies' man looking for a last resort? A phony?

Actually he was a little of each.

Oliver Jet had been a confidence man for thirty-five years, ever since quitting the solicitor to whom he was articled and being thrown out by his family, all because of telling an inheritor, for a consideration, what he was going to inherit. Oliver had visited top and bottom many times: owned lavish apartments and lived in garrety rooms, dined with Cafe Society's glitteringest and shared a sandwich with a sick whore, bought gold watches and pawned his only topcoat, been on amiable terms with the Royal Canadian Mounted Police's hierarchy and suffered through three eternities of imprisonment. His methods had ranged from peddling inferior brushes supposedly made by the blind to selling shares in mercury mines which he had sunk in his imagination, from writing begging letters to running a large-scale charity swindle.

Hundreds of men and women had he relieved of cash. Yet curiously enough, few bore him ill will. Most thought back with pleasure on the association. Oliver Jet was a charmer, and his charm had such a naturalness that it seemed impossible for it to be faked, to be merely his professional stock in trade. No victim could bring himself to fully accept Oliver as a crook. And in a way Oliver felt the same, for he owned, of all things, a conscience, one which told him that he had never taken from those who could not afford their loss, generally true, while the stronger cases he casuistrized to put the blame on his victim's avarice.

But there had been no victim now for six months—the time Oliver had been free following his last prison term, a year for what without his record might have been a civil matter, a breach-of-promise suit.

In six months he had done nothing, only borrowing a little here, leaving a bill for a week's lodging there, using his talent for the lowest ends until moving with his mistress into the home of Jonesy, the doughnut maker. Oliver had been waiting for Mr. or Mrs. Right to come along. It had been a long wait. It was still not over.

Was this a naturally bad town for marks, Oliver thought now, or was it something within himself that . . .

He thrust the thought down quickly, before the cold tinge of fear it brought could grow and insist on being recognized, faced. That his thrust succeeded was due not so much to his will's iron content as to the fact that already he was thinking about something else. Something Big.

Looking across the street at the doorway which led to the poolroom, he broke step nervously, faltering to a halt. Would any of the others be up there yet? he asked himself. Perhaps not. And if not, it would be wrong to go up, to appear too eager, even though eager he was—desperately. He had a position to maintain.

He walked on.

Opposite the Grand he turned in at the cocktail-lounge entrance of the Hotel Waterloo. Oliver had the pleasant, softly lit room to himself. He eased onto a stool at the bar and rapped for service. When a bartender came through from the beer parlor, Oliver, out of force of habit, bathed him in warmth with his eyes, smiled, and asked for a bottle of Carling's.

"Right you are, Mr. Wilson," the man said, also smiling.

Being remembered from past visits, false name and all, fed a boost to Oliver's spirits. He twitched his shoulders, rubbed his fattening nose, tipped a precious ten cents and when the barman had gone drank off half the ale. He turned to survey his surroundings with an attitude almost of grandeur.

He saw that he was not, after all, the only customer. At a side table sat a woman. Their eyes met briefly before the woman gave her attention back to stirring a drink.

13

Oliver examined the customer with interest. By the fact that she was of those best and longest years in a woman's life between thirty-nine and forty, by her hair style and clothes and cosmetics, he knew her to be a type with which he was more than familiar: reasonably educated, financially stable, divorced or separated or widowed, not averse to having a discreet lover; a type he had ofttimes dominated in mind, body, and bank account.

She glanced up again. He smiled faintly. As she looked away, she too smiled faintly.

She's on, he told himself with an urgent mental nudge. Go across.

His heart was suddenly beating fast and his stomach had gripped up and his temples felt tight.

Go. Go across with one of your dozen casual openings. Move in. This may be it. Mrs. Right.

Oliver sat tensely still, legs twined around the stool, the glass becoming slippery in his hand. He sat feeling sick and stupid. He sat and watched the woman glance his way a number of times while finishing her drink, gather her things together, get up, glance again, leave.

With a shudder he relaxed. He was sweating.

After taking his time about lighting a cigarette and tasting his ale, he was steady, if low. He felt old and tired.

Looking in the mirror behind the bar, he stared bleakly at the faint redness where his hair was tinted, the sagging flesh, the lines that ran across his brow.

He breathed out a soft sigh, remembering the face which mirrors had showed him in the past.

The next moment he looked away with a hiss of annoyance at his mood. He told himself he had changed hardly at all. If he was graying and scored with lines it was merely from worry. And he certainly had a lot to worry about.

First the possible caper with Erik and Lefty and Mr. Mortimer. That was number one. Even if it did come off, there was still the problem of a successful cover-up, followed in lesser degree by the fear that someone in the underworld might discover that he, Oliver Jet, had been involved in anything so boorish, so lacking in his renowned finesse.

There was the worry of keeping up to Jonesy and Pel the pretense of being at work on a swindle, parrying or ignoring Jonesy's endless hints about money and questions on when was the trap going to be sprung, and the degrading feeling from living on charity, even though it would be well repaid, the reluctant host having been promised a quarter of the mythical swindle's proceeds. Jonesy looked reproachful if an extra slice of bread were taken.

There was the worry about appearance. Every day saw his one suit grow a little shabbier, his linen grayer, his shoes more cracked.

There was the worry of being unable to begin even on outlines of the picture of luxury he had painted for Pel when he had talked her away from the counter of a village drugstore. Their present existence was completely opposite to what she had expected. It couldn't continue. Her patience surely had a limit.

And what about her and Jonesy. Would she, perhaps out of boredom, gravitate toward the younger man? More to the point, did it matter?

At once Oliver concluded that matter it did—although not in love with her, although often bored in her company —being objective enough to realize that she buttressed his ego, kept him young, assured him he was still able to attract and win a beautiful girl of twenty. It would be a blow to lose her, a greater blow losing her to the dense and ugly Jonesy.

Oliver thought with a sneer of his host's coarseness and background of petty crime, at the same time knowing he was doing so to hold down the greatest worry of all, which had been drawn out of the depths yet again by his lack of action minutes before.

Forgetting Jonesy, edging close to the worry, Oliver mused that in the old days he would not have let an opportunity like that slip by, regardless of what else he might have been working on. He would have picked up the woman if only for kicks, for the feeling of power it brought.

Abruptly he gave up the fight of many weeks. He sagged. He closed his eyes. He allowed the cold thought to ski through.

Had he lost his confidence?

A shattering question. It was tantamount to a test pilot wondering if his nerve was shot or a prima donna doubting the perfection of her range. It was shattering, yet Oliver thought on.

Had it vanished, the magic touch that had earned him thousands, enabled him to move with ease among people of every level, made it possible for him to talk his way out of trouble a hundred times and built him a reputation as the sharpest man in the game? If he was no longer sure of himself then he was finished. A confidence man without confidence was like a surgeon without a knife: the knowledge was there, the essential tool was missing.

Oliver opened his eyes tiredly and stared into space, regarding the question with horror but not attempting to reply.

He stayed thus for some time, until the bartender passed. He gave a smiling nod to Oliver—which was the very lift he needed.

Sitting up straight he blustered to himself that he was being ridiculous. A few months of inactivity . . . what was that? He deserved a rest after a year inside. With this woman, and the other people who might, *might* have come through as marks, he was simply being cautious, as befitted a three-time loser. He had, of course, some rust in the works, but the woman's willingness to flirt, his impression on the bartender, the fact of Pel—these showed he had lost nothing.

Oliver, half-convinced, shot a soiled cuff defensively and reached for his glass to dismiss the subject. His hand was trembling.

The glass, he saw, was empty. Remembering the puny state of his pocket he decided against a second beer. Anyway, he thought, looking at his watch, now it was time for the poolroom.

16

"Do you think Jet will come?" asked the Great Erik.

"Got an idea he will," Mr. Mortimer said.

They were standing on their respective sides of the counter, the owner showing his nervous excitement by drumming fingers, the man with the black eye patch not showing his by standing tensely straight.

Lefty Steel leaned back on the nearest table. He was living this moment, the mob meeting, to its gorgeous fullest. His eyebrows and half smile were whimsical-tough. He spun a coin repeatedly up and down, an act he had brought to perfection after months of practice during Chicago Period One.

The men were not talking. The poolhall was quiet. In his corner still sat the pensioner, and the evening's first customer had entered a moment before, a sallow youth who was wandering moodily between tables spinning ivories against the cushions.

Minutes passed. Mr. Mortimer drummed, Erik stood and Lefty went on being George Raft.

The swing doors twanged open. Everyone turned to watch the entrance of Oliver Jet. It was a good one. He paused, surveyed the hall, smiled distantly like an epicure in a cafeteria, lifted his chin and clasped his hands behind and strolled to the counter.

There were subdued greetings.

The host: "Oliver."

Erik, irked at the smooth entrance: "Jet."

Lefty: "Evening, Mr. Jet."

Oliver: "Good evening, gentlemen."

The youth who had been wandering around, hopefully followed the new arrival and came to a halt in the penumbra of the counter lights. He was stared at pointedly by the four men. He offered a loose smile.

To Lefty Steel, the confidence trickster said under his breath, "Shoo him off."

Although he had been rejoicing that his presence in such exalted company had an observer, Lefty was equally delighted to change audiences, show off to his colleagues.

Putting away his coin he pushed himself lazily from his

lean and swayed to the youth, whose expression dropped into blankness at finding a face loom close to his own.

"Get lost, you," Lefty said.

The youth drew back his head. With an angry frown he stuck out his chin. "Eh?"

A tremor of worry rattled Lefty's heart. This, he suddenly realized, was for real. Also, annoyingly, Lefty was worried that the other's feelings might be hurt.

He flinched, winked, softened his tone and said, "A bit of business, see."

After glancing at the others and giving Lefty a vicious look, the youth swung away, strolled off to the doors.

Lefty slid a relieved hand over his pimples before turning back to his place. He left the coin in his pocket.

"Well," Mr. Mortimer said, following a stammered clearing of his throat.

The meeting was on.

And no one had anything to say.

"*Well?*" asked the illusionist after a moment, a glare in his visible eye, an edge of impatience in his voice. "Has anyone thought of an idea?"

"Have you?" countered Mr. Mortimer, eyebrows hopeful.

"No."

"Nor I," said Oliver Jet, as though slightly amused, as though condescending to something not quite his style.

"Me neither," Lefty said. "But I'm working on it."

Erik gave the younger man a look of dislike before turning to the host. "Mr. Mortimer?"

"Me? No, I've not thought of anything."

In Oliver Jet's chest formed a hard lump of disappointment. "So," he said gruffly, "we're still in the same place."

The others gave slow nods. All fell silent, each thinking of the impasse.

These four unlikely associates in criminal intent had closed ranks slowly, over a period of weeks, so slowly that none now found any surprise in the association. Nor were they any longer surprised at the crime to which they aspired. Had it been broached cold, each would have rejected it with shock. Taking form gradually, the idea lost force, its criminality declining, and as time passed they grew inexorably wedded to the scheme by their various forms of need.

Pre-scheme, they had been aware of one another's existence only in the most casual way. Lefty had known his future partners as people to treat with deference, as, respectively, the poolroom boss, a stage celebrity, a genuine criminal (it soon being common knowledge around the tables that Oliver Jet had served time). Erik had played the con man occasional games of pool and drank the odd beer with him in the Hotel Waterloo while waiting to go onstage. Mr. Mortimer had known the others as customers.

Lefty it was who set the machinations in motion.

One day he met a girl who was struggling with a large suitcase. He carried it for her to the railroad depot, treated en route to a chattered résumé of her life as a domestic, her most recent position—just terminated—and her plans when she got back to Toronto. She enlarged with fury on her last employer, who, it seemed, was the world's rottenest bitch.

Lefty was only quarter-listening, was in fact regretting his instinctive offer of help. For one thing, the suitcase was tearingly heavy; for another, he was petrified lest people should take him for that horror of horrors, a tourist. After leaving the girl, however, one thing she had said stuck in his mind:

". . . arguing about my pay, the old bitch, when she's got half a million bucks in her safe."

This smidgen of smiling information he had whispered to Oliver Jet, doing the thing in style, taking the other out onto the poolhall stairway, his motive in telling being solely to get "in" and show that he too was one of the boys.

While unimpressed, there were always such stories floating about, Oliver made inquiries of Mr. Mortimer.

Yes, the old woman was known to be wealthy, but as for keeping actual cash on hand . . .

Perhaps Mr. Mortimer knew a way of checking?

Well, as a matter of fact, he did, and he would—for curiosity's sake of course.

Of course.

Quiet, cautious smiles.

Mr. Mortimer performed a subtle pumping on an acquaintance, a tradesman who delivered regularly to the home of Mrs. Vandle. He learned, and passed on to Oliver, what several people knew but kept to themselves, not wishing to be the imparters of so dangerous, so tempting a tidbit. Mrs. Vandle, seventy-two, widow of a broker, had in the bedroom which she rarely left a safe containing two hundred thousand dollars' worth of cash and jewelry, or so she surprisingly and foolishly intimated to her staff, which comprised a live-in maid, a daily cook, and a chauffeur cum bodyguard.

Oliver and Mr. Mortimer went to Lefty Steel, who told how he had come by the story and swore he had repeated it to no one else. All three agreed quietly that the situation was interesting.

Mr. Mortimer and Lefty, being local men, set out to build dossiers on Mrs. Vandle's female staff, while Oliver, following an idea of his own, gradually presented the case to the Great Erik and when the reaction was favorable asked was he familiar with the chauffeur, a Dave Morgan, who was known to have been in show business.

Dave Morgan? Big and strong? Crewcut? About thirty-five?

"Yes," said Oliver.

"Yes, I know him," said Erik.

Morgan, after some years of pro wrestling, had toured the theater circuit for two weak seasons with his own strong-man act, billing himself as David Goliath.

The plot was thickening to a nice consistency.

Erik contacted Dave Morgan. They met for short periods a number of times. Though reticent about his job, preferring to talk show biz, Morgan did let a few facts emerge. He had got the job by answering a newspaper ad some months before. His duties consisted in the main of simply being on the premises, a man about the house. He had a day off, but not a whole night. Mrs. Vandle liked an occasional drive. She was a semi-invalid, getting about in a chair or on sticks.

"Seems to me," Erik said, "that I've heard she has a lot of money in her safe, and keeps the key around her neck."

"Yeah?" said Morgan vaguely. He passed on to another subject.

The ex-wrestler, obviously, was going to play a coy game.

Meanwhile, the others had been finding out that the daily cook was taken to and from work on the back of a motorbike driven by her husband, a retired policeman; and that the new live-in maid went out only on her free afternoon, was saving to get married and thought her mistress a marvelous person—the latter facts gleaned by Oliver during a chat with the girl at a bus stop, after Lefty had failed dismally to pick her up.

All information was pooled at the billiards emporium, where the four now met every night to talk frankly, no longer pretending "interest" or "curiosity."

The cook and maid were ruled out. As potential fifth columnists they were made of poor stuff. And Morgan, Erik reported, was getting harder to corner, and when cornered clammed up at any mention of his job. Could be he was a loyal servant, could be he was suspicious.

Then came the impasse.

Oliver and Erik, walking one morning along the lakefront, ran into Mrs. Vandle's bodyguard. Before the duo could speak, Dave Morgan said, "You're Oliver Jet, aren't you?" Apparently he knew Oliver by sight and reputation from the con man's heyday in Toronto.

Following mumbled commonplaces, Dave Morgan, stiff and frowning, strode on. The next time he was telephoned by Erik he snapped that he was busy, and hung up. His suspicion was now a solid fact. The scheme trod water.

There seemed no way of getting around the ex-wrestler, and supposing there were, he would know where to point the finger if a robbery was committed. Morgan was in the way, had to be removed, yet none of the four schemers liked the obvious solution.

21

"There must be some alternative," said Oliver Jet with a touch of vehemence, forgetting his role of being above all this.

Mr. Mortimer shook his head. "I can't think of anything."

Lefty gave the Parisian shrug he had been working on lately. It came off rather well, except that no one was looking. He glanced behind. The pensioner wasn't looking either.

Erik rose to the crest of his toes, sank again and said, "One thing did occur to me. A bit clutching at strawsish."

"Yes?" asked the con man and the host.

"Might take time."

"Yes?" they asked again.

"The thing is, if we could get something on friend Morgan. You know."

"Mm," Mr. Mortimer said, avoiding anything as nasty as blackmail. "If there's anything to get."

Oliver had brightened. "That's not a bad idea, Erik. What about his past?"

"I know practically nothing about it. We were only theater acquaintances. No, what I had in mind was his present."

"Yes, I see. Perhaps he's involved with a married woman, or with something else he shouldn't be."

Mr. Mortimer said, "How could we find out though?"

"What about his movements?" asked the illusionist.

"Erratic," said Oliver.

Lefty, who had done most of the watching at Mrs. Vandle's, added, "Comes and goes at all different times, driving out in that big Caddy of the old bird's."

Mr. Mortimer asked, "Where does he go?"

"Shopping, or for a drink, or just away someplace, gone for hours. These long deals is at all different times, morning, afternoon, any goddamn time."

"Erratic," repeated the con man.

Mr. Mortimer said, "What about his day off?"

"Thursday that would be. Last week he did a long deal in the morning and then stayed home. This week he took a coupla fast trips into town and at night went to the movies."

"And when that happens," put in Erik, "going out in the evening, he calls a friend of the old girl's, a retired hospital matron, and she comes to visit with Mrs. Vandle till he gets back."

Oliver said, "So there're always at least two people on hand."

"Yes. He said Mrs. Vandle was nervous."

"Serves her right for bragging," said Lefty Steel thoughtlessly. He was wishing there were some of the regulars on hand to witness this impressive scene, starkly lit in the dim hall, this secret meeting of the mob, four hard men.

Mr. Mortimer said, "Er, I wonder where he goes when he's away a long time."

"We could follow him and find out," Erik said. "But my car's in the repair shop."

"We can always borrow one."

"My Uncle Stan," said Lefty. "He might lend me his car, he might. It's got a radio."

"I'll get a car," said Oliver, wishing to assert his authority. Immediately, he regretted speaking, for it would be a horrible loss of face if he failed to get the only vehicle he knew of, if Jonesy refused to loan his ramshackle panel truck.

He said, "Your uncle's car might be better though."

Lefty also regretted speaking. His uncle, he knew, would be more likely to loan his car to a nearsighted drunk. He said:

"Come to think of it, Uncle Stan's gone on vacation. Won't be back for a week."

"I think we should do this at once," said the man behind the counter. "First thing tomorrow."

Oliver betrayed nothing. "Very well. Who'll go with me?"

Because common sense told him to get involved physically as little as possible, Erik said he had an appointment, which was more or less true since he had just decided to take Miranda out to brunch. Mr. Mortimer had to look after the poolroom.

"I'll go with you then," Lefty said. "What's half a day's pay?"

"Nothing," said Erik, "compared to nearly a quarter of a million dollars."

Oliver clenched his fists, Erik smiled thinly, Mr. Mortimer sent his fingers into a mad drumming and Lefty wished again that some of the regulars could just see him now.

In a minute the meeting was over. They separated, these four hard men, each a degree more optimistic than on the previous night.

Beside the theater Erik turned into an alley narrow and dim, turning again after a short walk into a doorway topped by a swinging sign: Stage Door.

As he stepped inside, he shot his usual look of disapprobation at the dark empty cubbyhole where once had lurked that all-powerful figure, the stage door keeper. Sick and dying, the Grand no longer had need of one. The door was left open and the last out at night locked up. Erik disapproved strongly. Loving Theatre as he did, he was opposed to anything which undermined its mystique.

His face cleared when having walked up a concrete ramp he arrived backstage.

Backstage. The very word gave him a thrill. He never failed to feel elated whenever he entered that curious world, be it after an absence of only hours. Familiarity had not bled his awe.

He was in an oblong area, its tall ceiling out of sight in darkness. The near wall held wires and switches, the other supported an iron staircase to a catwalk. The wings took up one side, across were doors and a tunnel that led to dressing rooms.

Scattered about in the light from harsh naked bulbs were stage hands and performers who had the casualness imbued by a long-running show.

A bell rang, lights backstage clicked low, artistes and

24

workers dropped their voices, the safety curtain began its grumbling climb and the five-man pit orchestra limped into a swing version of *Greensleeves*. Intermission was over.

A comic in rags and his smartly dressed feed appeared from the tunnel, arguing in undertones. These opened the second half, Miranda followed, next came an Irish tenor, and to Erik belonged the final thirty minutes of the show.

The curtains parted. Abruptly ending their argument the comics strode to center stage, both laughing loudly. There was a polite stammer of applause.

Erik moved quietly through the gloom which echoed with the comics' voices and was sliced by tall shafts of light from the stage. Climbing the stairs he came onto the catwalk. It fronted three doors. Erik opened the one that bore a star. His dressing room was a concrete-cold place full of untidiness. Pinned around the mirror were the six well-wishing telegrams sent on opening night by his mother.

After hanging up his coat Erik sat down and removed his black eye patch. He blinked the uncovered eye.

The eye was normal, without fault, in function and appearance the equal to its mate. The role of the patch was purely cosmetic.

Erik had discovered many years before the value, to him, of a patch, when he bought one to hide a sty. Straight away he realized how the covering and its ribbon improved his appearance. His face became more masculine, less immature. He had gained a look of authority, not to mention mystery. He was suddenly attractive to women, prime material for an affair, a fascinating man who obviously had a past. The sty died and the patch lived on.

With tie off and collar loosened, Erik began to make-up. When his face was covered with color he reached for a black pencil.

He paused on hearing from the orchestra a chord he recognized. The comics were going into the song which closed their act. Erik went out of his room just as Miranda was coming out of hers.

Miranda was strikingly pretty, in the way associated with the pictures on boxes of candy. Petite, blond hair swept up to a tiara, wearing a white, sequined cape, she seemed unreal, untouchable, like the fairy atop a Christmas tree. Her small all-eyes face looked innocent; looked too good, too pretty and too delicate to kiss. Miranda was every schoolboy's dream of feminine perfection.

She had an offstage smile, an elfin one-sided smile, which appeared to say, "I know, it's all a bit icky, but a girl has to make a living."

As usual, on seeing his fiancée Erik felt a warm movement under his heart. The gloom of the upper level, making her whiteness ethereal, intensified his emotion.

"Hello, darling," she said softly.

He swallowed, dipping his head. "Good evening, Miranda."

"Not changed yet?"

"About to. You're looking very beautiful tonight."

"Thank you. Do you love me?"

"I love you."

They held hands, the most they dare while wearing make-up. Until applause announced the previous act's finale they talked, of the early night they both needed, of tomorrow's brunch date.

Miranda went lightly down the stairway. One minute later she came flashingly in and out of view beyond the wings, twirling around in a time-killing dance before going into her routine.

Erik smiled. His feeling of love now reached its highest pitch. Although unaware of the fact, this was how he liked Miranda most: something glittering in the distance, a daydream, a promise which need never be fulfilled.

With difficulty he turned away to finish dressing.

The living room above the doughnut shop had jazzy wallpaper, a TV console, a suite of imitation leather that had worn to gray fabric on the arms and a center table holding a plaster boy forever on the point of eating a plaster cherry.

In a chair lounged Jonesy, on the couch sat Pel. They were lost in a television play.

Jonesy was fair and forty. His face was plain, though not unpleasant, and its openness showed that he had a sense of humor. Tall and slim, he wore neat slacks and a blue sweater with green darns.

He glared at the screen while trying with tortured twists of head and fist to gnaw fingernails that were no longer gnawable.

Pel was also tall, also fair. Long waves fell to the broad shoulders of a figure which was good enough to be too full to model clothes. Despite Oliver Jet's conviction, Pel had no beauty. Her face was attractive in a young, twenty-year-old way; it would become nothing inside a decade. Her only make-up was the heavy Egyptian bit around her eyes.

The play came to an end. Jonesy turned down the volume on a news broadcast as he rose and stepped to the table to light a cigarette. Pel picked up her paperback. A train moved slowly past, dithering the room.

Sitting again, Jonesy fell to musing on the male half of his house guests. With a sad blink he thought how different Oliver was from what he'd always believed. It was sort of disappointing.

When Jonesy had been a youth in Toronto, the name Oliver Jet had had a magic quality to the habitués of the poolrooms, coffee shops, dances, and street corners. It meant glowing success, the apex of cleverness, the last word in style. Women were mad for him, big men dropped his name, there was a Jet lapel. Anyone who had spoken to him was envied and those who could claim acquaintance were of the *élite*. His exploits were recounted with gusto and wonder, more so those of how he had avoided arrest than those of his capers, the vast proceeds of which were too much to imagine. His mannerisms were aped—the quizzical eyebrow and the head tilted back to exhale when smoking—and his sayings repeated: the clever man knows everything, the shrewd man knows everyone.

It was said that a famous actress was his mistress, that he was wanted by Interpol, that he vacationed in Paris and Rome in his own fabulous villas, that he always carried at least a thousand dollars. He would be seen sometimes tooling by in a magnificent car. And sometimes he would saunter into a bar with a group of friends, drinking black velvet until, as word got around that O.J. was here, the place began to get too full. He was a minor legend at thirty-five.

With the passing of time he was seen less and less in Ontario. He became almost a myth. Whenever a big swindle hit the papers it was said that he was the string-puller. Rumor had it that he was in the States running the Capone empire, had been seen dining in Ottawa with the Governor General, was fleecing the casinos of Europe with a foolproof system, had pulled the biggest con caper in history and was living like a king in the Argentine. Once when it was known for an absolute fact that he was serving eighteen months in Vancouver it was treated with reverence because they said it wasn't for anything he himself had done, he was taking the rap for a friend, which, they said, was just like him, always true to the code, one of the boys. He became more of a legend than ever.

On meeting him by accident in Marlake, Jonesy had been flattered and eager when Oliver, saying he was temporarily out of funds, offered to cut him in on a caper in exchange for board and a little financial help. Jonesy gladly agreed. But after some weeks he felt differently. He was tired of doling out money, sick of Oliver's complaints about the accommodations, fed up with his irritableness. It was a disillusionment to have *the* Oliver Jet revealed as an ordinary man like anyone else. Furthermore Jonesy was bored with oft-repeated stories of capers, capers which, though most likely exaggerated, were still nowhere near as big as rumor had led him to suppose. And the latest one seemed to be going on forever. It was making Jonesy nervous. Hadn't Oliver once said that a caper should be like a love affair, quick and fierce, ended before it could become stale? If Oliver had lost his touch he could easily make a slip that would land them all in trouble. Which would mean the end of the comfortable legit life Jonesy had been living since renting the doughnut shop.

Jonesy stabbed out his cigarette. He wasn't happy with the situation. He wasn't happy at all.

It wouldn't be so bad, he thought sourly, if he could get somewhere with Pel. But she acted as if she was married to Oliver lousy Jet instead of only shacking up with him. A different approach would have to be tried. Deeds, not words.

He looked over at the blond girl. She was leaning forward as she read. Her peasant blouse hung low. Jonesy moved his head to get a better sighting on the cleavage.

Becoming conscious of the stare, Pel glanced up: then leaned back, flushing. She said, "Yes?"

"Er, I was wondering . . ."

"Yes?"

Jonesy became stern. "Listen, has Oliver told you what kind of a swindle he's working on?"

"No."

"Well, has he told you when he's going to bring it off?" She shook her hair.

"Yeah," Jonesy said. "Maybe he's already tried and come a cropper."

"No he hasn't. Don't worry, they don't make 'em no smarter than Ollie."

"I dunno. Maybe he's lost the touch. He's getting on."

"Forty-seven isn't old."

Jonesy laughed. "Forty-seven? Come on. Oliver Jet's fifty-five if he's a day."

"Oh, he is not."

"Anyway," Jonesy said in a softer tone, "he's too old for a kid like you."

Pel looked down at her fingernails. "Ollie's the only man I'm interested in."

Jonesy grinned as his eyes strayed back to the neck of Pel's blouse. "Changing the subject to two others, I'll bet you don't wear falsies, do you?"

"Good night," she said, rising.

Much later, Oliver Jet was wending his solitary way home, a quiet, almost mournful figure who seemed oblivious to the resort's late evening bustle.

He had been to an outlying hotel where, as he was supposedly dining with the swindle's mark, there would be no chance of meeting Jonesy should be decide to go out for a drink. Oliver had sat for a long time over two beers, growing depressed by his inability to buy a few strong, cheering drinks, which caused him to feel disenchanted with the whole of the present outlook, which increased his craving for the drinks strong and cheering he was unable to buy. He hated himself.

Now he was musing that the scheme with Erik and the others didn't have a hope. It was too full of ifs. *If* he managed to borrow Jonesy's panel truck, *if* he was able to follow the big fast Caddy every time it went out, *if* on one of these times Morgan led the way to a smell, *if* the smell was bad enough to bring Morgan to heel, *if* . . .

Not only was the scheme futile, his partners were a mess. Lefty Steel, pimple farmer, seemed to be living in a world all his own. Erik was a prig with a capital F who had the personality of a dead tree. And Mr. Mortimer, although a decent enough soul, his meekness suggested collapse under the slightest strain. Three more unsuitable men would be hard to find. A mess.

Oliver turned into Waterloo Street. He let himself into the shop and went up the narrow, enclosed staircase quietly. Why quietly? he wondered.

The living room was deserted. From behind one door came the sound of snoring, to which Oliver listened with care, trying to judge if it were genuine. Jonesy was not usually so early abed. Unable to tell if the snore was real or pretend, Oliver went into the other bedroom and clicked on the light.

There was a silent mound under the blankets. "Pel?" No answer. Since she could hardly be tired out from her performance as a housewife, Oliver wondered as he began to undress if she was tired out from a performance of another kind, satiated, and for that reason feigning sleep. Or was it himself? Did he fear he was losing his grip in all things?

He looked in a mirror, an act which, he realized, was growing into something of a habit. His face was lined with tiredness, the eyes red, the flesh saggy. Tilting back his head to remove the double chin, however, he told himself he definitely did not look fifty-four and was still handsome. But he knew that the strain of the possible robbery was telling. If it could only be concluded soon. Then a long holiday. After that, well, perhaps it would be time to think about retirement. In Toronto, where he was known. He could let it out with a wink that he was still working, commuting over the line. He could stroll around like a lord, Pel on his arm.

Cheered by this warm vision, Oliver finished undressing, put out the light and fumbled his way into bed. Pel stirred. He touched her shoulder and spoke her name. She turned, mumbling sleepily. He knew she wasn't acting. "Nothing," he said. "It's all right. Go to sleep."

For the fourteenth time Lefty Steel walked along the lakeshore in front of the concentration of amusements. His shoulders were in a villain slouch, his hands were deep in his jacket pockets. He walked slowly yet with purpose, face severe and narrowed eyes fixed firmly ahead. He looked to be on his way to a date with danger. Or so he thought. In reality, to those who in the dense crowd of drunk and vacation-giggly, ice-cream lickers and eaters of french fries from paper cones, to those who became passingly aware of Lefty he looked as if he were bending every faculty to the control of his stomach until he could find a place to vomit.

The evening he had spent playing pool and going every fifteen minutes to the counter, where he would whisper with urgent manner something of inconsequence into Mr. Mortimer's ear, which certainly showed everyone how very in he was. He lost seven straight games.

Afterward, taking as it were a nightcap, he had set out to do what he so often did: stroll along the lakefront and let himself be seen.

Now at last he was surfeited. Instead of turning back again at the end of the amusements he kept going and went into Waterloo Street.

His pose fell away. Already he was thinking about the

morning, seeing himself and Oliver Jet roaring along in a big black car in tire-screaming pursuit of a Cadillac.

Near the railroad line Lefty entered one of the brick houses which faced the store of J. Jones, went along a black passage and into a kitchen whose stark cleanliness, neatness, and lack of spiritual warmth told what it sorely missed, the feminine touch.

At the table sat Lefty's father, a man of fifty in overalls. His worn face was slack from its nightly quota of beer, plus the final, frantic, not-stoned-yet two or three whiskies.

"'Lo, Ronald," he said. "Got a butt?"

Lefty eyed him with distaste as he tossed a cigarette across. He didn't understand the attraction of alcohol, didn't know how greatly it could comfort failures or those to whom failure came naturally. He thought addiction itself was the failing, in all cases.

He found a slice of bread and butter, which he stuffed in his mouth while sitting to take off his shoes and socks.

Trying not to sound drunk, the elder Steel asked, "Been out with the girls?"

Lefty winked. The other cackled, pleased to be on friendly terms with his son.

Lefty's wink was a lie. He had never been out with a girl, never possessed a woman. He carried on a love affair with himself, in every sense, due to a self-identification with those same idols whom he worshiped.

"Nice stuff around, eh?" his father said with a widower's sigh. "All them tourist girls."

"Yeah."

"Bet they're pretty easy, eh?"

Lefty tossed his footwear into a corner. "I'm off to bed." He rose and padded along the passage. In his bedroom he clicked life to a naked bulb and bolted the door.

The walls held action pictures clipped from magazines, a drawing by Lefty of Dillinger's capture, posters of gangster movies he had peeled from wet billboards, and a signed glossy of Edward G. Robinson.

After putting his jacket on a chair back, Lefty knelt and from beneath the bed pulled out a suitcase, which he un-

32

locked. From among the jumble inside he took a box and from the box took a gun, a .22.

He had bought the revolver years before, from a boy who claimed to have found it on the beach. The chambers had been full, nine bullets; now there were eight; one glorious day Lefty had gone out in the woods to test his treasure, thrilled yet sad at expending one of its golden eggs.

Now from the suitcase he brought a shoulder holster which he had made himself. He slipped the harness on and put the revolver into its pouch. Standing, he lit a cigarette, unbuttoned his collar, loosened his tie and turned to face the dresser mirror.

The picture was perfect. Sallow young man with gun, eyes slitted and cigarette dangling, bare room of a thousand Hollywood underworld hotels.

Lefty moved back and leaned sneeringly against the wall. He stared at his reflection. And he stared . . .

Flashing neons penetrated his room. From the city street many floors below came the roar of traffic, from somewhere in the distance came the wail of a police siren, from the room next door came strident jazz, a woman's laugh, the clink of glasses. Lefty waited unruffled. He didn't care that his life was in danger. They didn't make them any tougher than Lefty Steel. Soon the mob would be here with the roadster and they'd all blow town, hole up someplace for a while and then pull another job.

Lefty tensed. The siren had grown louder. Now it moaned into silence close by. Instinct told him that this was it. He was in trouble. Someone had turned stoolie. He could almost see the G-men getting out of the car, hurrying inside, crowding into the elevator and zooming up. Grim-faced they enter the corridor, bringing out their guns and walking softly. This was it all right. But Lefty didn't turn a hair. He smiled as he reached a hand to his holster . . .

There was a knock on the door.

Lefty jerked around, his mouth flabbing open. He felt suddenly dizzy, as though he had just stopped twirling.

"Ronald?" called a voice.

Lefty reeled to the bed and sat. He brought both hands to his damp brow. The confusion cleared enough for him to understand that his father was outside. He asked, "What?"

"Just saying good night. Something wrong?"

"I—er—I was asleep."

"The light's on."

"I forgot it. Good night."

"Night." A door opened and closed.

Lefty shook his head to clear away the last of the dizziness. He thought he must have been dozing off.

Seeing he still wore holster and gun he took them off and put them away. With a mighty, happy yawn he began to undress.

The room was in one of those no-star motels which rent accommodation by the night or by the hour or by the fifteen minutes; motels which ask no questions, give no service and smell of furtiveness; motels which titillate the salacious, cause true lovers to grow ashamed and make even bona fide honeymooners feel dirty.

The room had a bed and a table. The table was piled with clothing. On the bed lay a blonde, on the blonde lay a man. The man was asleep.

Her slight difficulty in breathing and the weight the blonde didn't mind. She found her position a comfort, satisfying. And the sex of a few minutes before had been satisfying too. She had needed it badly. A week had passed since the last meeting. A week was a long time. Still, she was now partly eased, and soon he would wake up and they would start again. They would kiss hot kisses, hard, growing more violent. His strong hands would probe, almost cruelly. He would make her repeat his gutter words. He would insult her by calling her a show biz whore and praise her by saying she had great contortions. She would be crushed, bruised, thrilled beyond words. When he woke up.

She turned her head and bit Dave Morgan's neck.

TWO

It was a bright shrill morning. At half-past eight the town was astir, save for those enterprises concerned with entertainment, which were faintly sordid in sleep. Along Waterloo Street a milkman made as much noise as he could, a maid swilled down the hotel's frontage of sidewalk, a green panel truck creaked its way out and a bicycle was ridden slowly in.

Mr. Mortimer dismounted with a wobble and wheeled to a large door, which he unlocked and set open with a wedge. He put his bicycle inside, applying a lock against theft. Up the steps he went and through the swing doors into darkness. He smiled at coming home.

Unerringly picking his unseen way he crossed to the counter and switched on its light, bathing himself in glory and bringing long-shadowed life to every corner of the hall. He passed around a slow look, still smiling, before setting about his chores.

At nine o'clock the tea urn was steaming with vigor, Mr. Mortimer was meticulously cutting sandwiches, and Mrs. Chaps the char was mopping the linoleum.

Forty-odd, small and cheerfully energetic, hair pulled back into a bun, the widow Chaps had a round face with red cheeks, a sweet smile and eyes full of naïveté, a face that made you think of Grandma Moses, hot buttered toast, patchwork quilts. Mrs. Chaps liked an occasional Guinness, movies you could have a good cry at, and Mr. Mortimer, whose linoleum she had been mopping for seven years.

Loudly humming *Lili of Laguna* as she worked, her

thoughts were on the film she had seen the night before.

Mr. Mortimer's thoughts were on his associates. He wondered if Oliver Jet and Lefty Steel, in the green van, were still watching Mrs. Vandle's, or were they already following Morgan. And what, if anything, would come of it? Would . . . ? But there was no point in conjecture.

He began to think of his associates themselves. He knew little about the three men. Lefty he had been aware of for years as one of the young poolroom types who sprawled around the tables and treated the boss of their haunt with an unnecessary amount of respect—which Mr. Mortimer admitted he enjoyed. He knew Lefty lived in Waterloo Street and did unskilled work. Of his hopes and feelings he knew nothing. He decided, however, that Lefty was a nice young man, a decent lad, and if he liked to strut and pose a bit, so what. He was only a kid after all. Yes, Lefty was okay.

Erik now, he was something else. You couldn't tell *what* went on behind that impassive façade. He rarely smiled or frowned. This, though breeding dislike, gave you confidence in the man. He was sure of himself, made a perfect ally, would prove coldly efficient when others were getting flustered. He would never be a buddy, but a more reliable partner would be hard to come across.

Oliver Jet. There was a man of success. From hints he had dropped it was clear that he had recently engineered a big swindle and was now lying low before starting another. The fact that while obviously a man of wealth he was living as if quite poor showed cleverness. A real brain. They were lucky to get him. He was likable as well, maybe a sentimentalist underneath, but as far as friendship went, that was out. You could never, for instance, ask him into your home, because he was, after all, a crook.

In a moment, having finished with his colleagues, and neatly skipping over the actual crime, Mr. Mortimer's thoughts turned to the future. He smiled tremulously and his stomach quailed.

With alarm he saw that lack of concentration had caused him to cut a slice of cheese to a thickness of a quarter inch.

36

Deferring work he leaned folded arms on the counter and prepared to give himself up to his ambition.

What stopped him was noticing Mrs. Chaps.

He wondered what she would say if she knew. He had never told anyone, and he would like to. At times, keeping it to himself became unbearable. Not that there was any need for secrecy. It was just that the ambition was so close to his heart, so much a part of him that it could be imparted only to someone special.

And did Mrs. Chaps fit that category?

Mr. Mortimer thought she probably did. After all, the only ones he knew better were . . .

After a search of his mind Mr. Mortimer realized there was no one closer to him in the world than Mrs. Chaps, which brought him some surprise, plus more than a little hurt.

So, he thought. Mrs. Chaps was the one. Now was the time.

A tingle of excitement in his belly he left the counter and walked to where Mrs. Chaps was mopping between tables two and three. "Well!" he said brightly.

"Well!" the char smiled, stopping work and cuddling the handle of her mop.

Mr. Mortimer leaned his rump against a table. "Mrs. Chaps," he asked, gazing around, "what d'you think of the old place?"

Loyal, she said, "Fine, Mr. Mortimer, fine."

"Not bad, I suppose. But it's only a steppingstone. I won't always be here."

"Is that right?"

"Yes, Mrs. Chaps. I, you see, am a man of ideas."

"Ooh."

"I foresee something quite startling in my future. I'm not a man to mark time."

"I should think not." Her expression showed that the very idea was ridiculous.

"Someday, therefore, if all goes well, I might find myself in quite different surroundings."

"Ah."

"At the moment it's all in my head, yet I don't doubt that someday my plan will come to life."

"Yes," she said, holding the handle tight and edging closer. "What's the plan?"

"I'm going to tell you, Mrs. Chaps. I want you to be the first to know."

"Thanks a lot. Yes?"

"I am going to create," Mr. Mortimer said slowly, looking away into a misty distance, "I am going to create a billiards palace. A super de-luxe, first class, A.1. hall with"—pausing—"with fifty tables."

Mrs. Chaps drew in a long breath. "Fifty tables!"

Nodding heavily, Mr. Mortimer talked on in a low voice, describing his ambition in all its glorious detail, seeing and making his listener see the tile floor, paneled walls, uniformed score-markers, chromium cue cases, extensive counter serving all manner of refreshments, the outside sign of neon which announced MORTIMER'S BILLIARDS PALACE, 50 TABLES 50, and those tables themselves, stretched out in a seemingly endless line, lights brilliant on their polished mahogany and coats of emerald green.

Finished, he sighed into silence. His lips wore a faint, poignant smile. His eyes were moist.

Mrs. Chaps stared at him with her head on one side, her mouth partly open, her expression one of awe in the presence of greatness. She reached out a hand, extended one finger, gently touched his arm and whispered, "You're a man with a dream, Mr. Mortimer. You're a man with a dream."

The house of Mrs. Vandle stood in a quiet suburb, facing the prettiness of a golf course, lying a hundred feet back from the separating road and the same distance from its neighbors. Denoting financial complacency rather than overwealth, aged about thirty, the house was a two-story affair of ornamental brick, bay windows, and one imitation turret. From the front of the unfenced lawn a drive of gravel swept by the side of the house, where the main door was located, to feed into a Tudoresque garage.

House and garage could be seen plainly from across and along the road at a point where a cutting ran into the young trees which sided the golf course. Parked in the cutting was an ancient green panel truck with body inscribed to the effect that J. Jones was the man to see for all your doughnut needs.

Lefty and Oliver had been waiting for an hour. They had talked little. Oliver had smoked three of his own cigarettes and four of Lefty's.

The younger man was brooding about the panel truck. He had expected something cool, not a wreck with loose floorboards and a missing window. That Oliver Jet, in answer to a grumble, had said this was preferable to the expensive sedans he could have got because it was so ordinary, made no difference. The van was all wrong. Lefty felt unsettled.

Oliver too was brooding about the truck, or at least, about Jonesy's reluctance to give it into his care. Jonesy had acted as if the thing were a T-Bird, had hummed and harred before agreeing and had repeated the endless instructions on how to treat the delicate transmission.

Oliver tutted with disgust. Jonesy, he thought, was a poor specimen. It was tragic that he had been promised a share of the caper. He deserved an obese nothing. But a promise, unfortunately, was a promise.

The two men sat on, each deep in his own brood, until a movement at the side of the Vandle house brought them upright and alert. A man had appeared.

Dave Morgan was big, a couple of inches over six feet and not an ounce under two hundred and twenty pounds. In ten years he would be fatally fat; he already owned a respectable paunch. His ruddy face, lumpily plain, was topped by a crewcut which, not bristling proudly as a crewcut should, lolled and spiked like the pile of a cheap rug.

"There he is," said Lefty, whispering.

"Quite," said Oliver.

The manservant went into the garage. Two minutes later he reappeared at the wheel of a brown Cadillac, drove out onto the road and headed toward the observation post.

39

The watchers lowered their heads, Oliver at the same time switching on and pressing the starter. The van grumbled to life, the sedan swept by, Oliver engaged gear and followed.

"Well," Lefty said from the side of his mouth, "he ain't going into town this morning, not this way he ain't."

"Then he might be going somewhere more interesting."

Lefty winked. He went back to wondering if his employer would take kindly to the permissionless time off.

Dave Morgan drove along the quiet suburban roads, spurting to fifty between bouts of caution at crossings. Keeping to a steady speed, Oliver held a satisfactory distance between the Cadillac and the van.

Soon Morgan left the residential area. At a junction he turned onto a busy road lined with stores. Oliver, for safety's sake, allowed himself to become separated by other vehicles from the car in front.

"Where does this road lead?" he asked.

"Out of town," Lefty said. "A few miles on it meets the highway between Windsor and Hamilton."

The Cadillac pulled into a service station. Oliver went on past and drew to a stop in the curb.

Lefty looked behind. "Let's hope he don't turn and go back again."

Oliver said, "Let's hope he isn't filling up to make a long trip, maybe Windsor."

"Yeah. He'd soon lose us in this crate."

Which is not what Oliver meant, even though he said, "Exactly." He meant there was not much fuel in the tank, not much money in his pocket. Should the journey be long, he would have to ask Lefty to buy gas. The thought made him shudder.

Abruptly, Oliver's expression changed. He smiled and his brow's burden of lines was eased. He looked a decade younger.

His mind had produced one of its many treasures. The setting was Toronto, the time some fifteen years before, the protagonist himself. He was walking along Bloor Street on a balmy afternoon. Earlier he had come up from Buffalo after cashing a mark's check for three thousand dollars, and had gone to the races, where, despite foolish betting, he had finished up another fifty dollars to the good. He felt like a king as he strolled in the sun. He could do anything he wanted. On an impulse he brought bills from his pocket and thrust them into the hand of a shabby man leaning by a beer parlor door, saying, "Have a drink on Oliver Jet." Seconds later he found himself doing the same with another man; then another. He continued handing out money all along the street, to loungers and passers-by, male or female, poor-seeming or otherwise, telling each recipient, "I'm Oliver Jet. Buy yourself a little something."

He embraced the memory. It was sweet. A wonderful day that had been. He never knew how much he had given away, and didn't care. He was on top. He was in the prime of life, had pulled a beautiful caper, the sun was warm and the future mellow. He was right up there on top.

And, thought Oliver, he would be up there again. Just as he had been up and down in the past, before and after that day, he would make the same trip many times in the years ahead. Now it was down, so the next move had to be up.

His face retained some of the glow brought by the memory. He was more cheerful than he had been in weeks. The mood was firmly set ten minutes later when Dave Morgan, having left the gas station, reached the highway and turned not toward Windsor but Hamilton.

In the room above the doughnut store a radio blared soul music, to which Pel hummed and swayed her tall body while making flicks with a duster. Hearing footsteps, she sat at the table, where she felt safer. She looked down at an open magazine.

The stairway door swung in to admit Jonesy. "I'm taking five," he said. He lit a cigarette.

Pel said, "Give us a one, Jonesy."

He tossed her cigarettes and matches. While watching her light up he wondered if he should broach what he had been thinking of for days. The question was not so much

41

would she go for the idea as would she tell Oliver about it.

"What you reading?" he asked to set things in motion.

"A story. It's about this ballet dancer that's in love with an army captain, but he doesn't like her at all." She went on to tell the plot, in which Jonesy found himself quite interested.

Pel concluded with, "You can usually tell what'll happen in these stories."

He saw his opening. "You like to read them though."

"Oh sure."

"Like a bit of love, eh?"

Pel looked down and started to trace a fingernail over a picture in the magazine.

Jonesy, encouraged by her silence, said, "But you need a younger man for that."

Knowing she should stop him before he went too far, but thinking it was better than cleaning or reading some old story, Pel shrugged, rose, and went to the sideboard ashtray.

Jonesy looked at the tight sweater and jeans. It seemed ridiculous that this should be for Oliver only, more ridiculous that she should want Oliver only. He said, "I like the way you walk."

Although she decided not to answer, Pel was pleased, thought it nice to be complimented, be desired. Oliver had been too preoccupied lately to pay her much attention. She sat again, lowering herself with particular smoothness.

"You should've been a model, Pel."

"Well, as a matter of fact, I was going to be once. Everyone said I should. They said I was a natural. And I do have the height."

"You'd've been a big hit."

"Yes," she said wistfully.

"A sensation."

She nodded, lost in imagination, seeing herself in a spotlight and hearing an audience gasp at her beautiful dress.

Jonesy could tell by her face what she was thinking. He said, "This life's a bit different, isn't it? No bright lights, nothing fancy to wear. You hardly ever go out even."

42

Pel returned from her dream. "Yes, it's a bit different."

"Too bad, I reckon. A beautiful girl like you, you should have lots of nice things, be taken about, night clubs, races, stuff like that. Not be stuck in a crummy room."

"Oh, this isn't a bad place, Jonesy."

Dismissing the flat with a wave, he tapped himself on the chest. "Me, I've got big plans."

Pel looked at him attentively. "Oh?"

He stepped to the table and rested on his elbows. Voice low, he asked, "Pel, would you answer me a question?"

"Sure." Her voice matched his.

"The only reason I'm asking is because I like you a lot, Pel. I think you're a great kid."

"Well," she said cautiously, "I like you too, Jonesy. What you want to ask me?"

"This. Are you in love with Oliver?"

Surprised at the question, and not sure of her answer, Pel looked down and began again to trace over the picture. As expected, the situation had reached a sticky point.

"What d'you say, eh?" asked Jonesy.

From below came a clang as the shop door was opened. Jonesy stood upright. He felt pleased with himself. Let her chew it over for a while, he thought. "Pel," he said, moving away, "I think you and me is going to reach an understanding."

Erik sat in the lounge of a boardinghouse, waiting for Miranda. He was a visitor here. Though he would have liked to have been a resident, he preferred to lean with convention and lodge in a house different from that in which Miranda stayed. They made love in Erik's room, with many precautions and with the window closely draped to help Erik's shyness of the before and after the act. He had no wish to see Miranda or have her see him dishabille. He was rather nervous of familiarity.

At female length Miranda appeared. Erik kissed her first on both cheeks, second on the hand, third on the lips. Miranda glittered.

Leaving, they walked along the street, chatting almost

unconsciously, knowing they made a striking couple and aware of the looks from passers-by and therefore acting a little.

After turning onto another street they settled from the first flush of togetherness limelight. Their talk became more substantial. Miranda asked, "Any news of your grandfather?"

For perhaps three seconds Erik failed to understand. Then he remembered that in paving the way for a possible success in crime he had invented a wealthy grandparent who was gravely ill.

He said, "No change. I telephoned Quebec this morning."

"What's wrong with him exactly?"

"Let's not talk about the old boy," Erik said. "Every time I do, I get the feeling I'm looking forward to a funeral."

"No need to feel that way. At his age there's no tragedy in dying. You've a perfect right to look forward to your inheritance."

"I suppose so."

"If I had lots of money coming to me I'd be giddy with joy."

"You have, darling. When we're married, what's mine will be yours."

She squeezed his arm.

"That is," he went on, "if the old boy leaves what I expect. He might be as poor as a church mouse."

"Either way, we'll be happy, won't we?"

"Yes, but we'll be even happier if we're able to do what we planned."

"True, darling."

What they planned was retirement for one, show business power for the other. Miranda knew her limitations, knew that her routine had small hope of advancement, knew that her freak joints would be yawn-makers were it not for her beauty and the imagination of the audiences' male element. TV was out: one exposure would suffice. Foreign tours were graveyards. She was not, in any case, as great a lover of greasepaint as Erik, so would not be too unhappy at becoming a mere wife. And she was twenty-eight.

Erik's theatrical future was also bleak, but with the necessary funds he could open his own private theater—a night club. Its floor shows would consist of the usual supporting acts, its headliner would always be an illusionist, himself and other top names. Attached would be a workshop and sales. He would try to get his place accepted as the headquarters of the Magic Circle, Ontario Chapter, then perhaps Canadian HQ, last perhaps North American HQ. The club would be unique, the spiritual home of all magicians. And he would be top dog.

His idea afforded Erik a thrill far superior to anything possible onstage. Already he could see his name appearing under articles, see himself presenting his new illusions at conferences and being repeatedly voted president.

Erik strolled smiling beside Miranda, who would, he had long since decided, make the perfect consort for a Man of Prominence.

Miranda was talking, her words vague to Erik in his happy thoughts. Abruptly, however, something she said, a name, acted on him like a slap with a wet cloth.

The name was Dave Morgan.

He stopped walking. "What?"

Miranda also stopped, surprised. "Mmm?"

"Who did you say?"

"Dave Morgan, dear. He billed himself as David Goliath."

Erik's breathing felt tight. "But what about him?"

"I've been telling you. Weren't you listening?"

"Well . . ."

"And for goodness' sake," she said with a laugh, "why're you looking so shocked?"

He forced a smile and took Miranda's arm. They walked on. "I was thinking about a new trick," he said. "Please tell me what you were saying."

"Dave Morgan. You remember. Strong-man act."

"Of course."

"He's here in Marlake, and guess what, he's working as a chauffeur!"

"How did you come to know Morgan?"

"We were on a couple of charity shows together, two seasons ago. But imagine, Erik, a chauffeur!"

"You knew him well?"

She shrugged prettily. "I suppose so. He took me out once."

"Oh?"

"Don't make noises like that," she giggled. "It was one time. Nothing happened. We shook hands."

Rattled by Miranda's knowing Morgan, and working on his next question, Erik was silent.

Not giggling, Miranda said, "It's true, dear. We shook hands. You're not going to be silly and jealous, are you?"

"No. When was it you met him here in town?"

"Three or four weeks ago. I bumped into him on the street."

"You didn't tell me."

"I forgot, dear, that's all, and I wasn't sure you knew him."

"I do. I've met him here several times. He didn't mention seeing you."

"Oh-oh. You *are* going to be jealous."

"What did you talk about?"

"Men are so silly," she told the sky.

Erik persisted. "What did you talk about?"

"Show biz, darling. He's still real interested. Pure ham at heart."

"How long were you talking? Did you go for a drink?"

"We simply stood there and chatted for a while," Miranda said lightly.

Erik decided to play up the jealousy angle. It would make his interest in Morgan seem natural and make Miranda avoid the strong man should she see him again. He further decided after more questions that there was nothing to worry about; she had met Morgan once only and he had mentioned neither Erik nor Oliver Jet.

46

He let the topic lapse until they were entering a cafe, when he asked, "You're sure you only shook hands?"

The invisible towline between purring limousine and limping panel truck began to stretch: the lead car had signaled for a turn, the van had circumspectly reduced speed.

They were in the shopping district of an outer suburb of Hamilton. Lefty it was, his head out of the glassless window to see beyond the intervening cars, who had warned of the Cadillac's blinking taillight.

Oliver said, "That's an alley he's going into. We daren't follow him there."

"Park then, and I'll tail him on foot."

"Just what I was about to suggest."

"Well, come on. There he goes."

The brown car went from sight. Oliver hustled the van into a parking space. Lefty hurriedly got out, sprinted across the road and into the alley.

Midway along he saw that the alley led only to a parking lot belonging to the movie house beside which it squeezed. At the end, gasping with excitement and the resentfulness of his lungs, he stopped and peeped around the corner. There were a dozen parked cars, one the Cadillac, from which Dave Morgan was alighting.

Lefty flattened himself against the wall. With head at a fierce angle he showed the parking lot one eye. He was elated, his earlier disappointment in transportation forgotten. This was the real thing.

The following moment Lefty was taken out of himself by surprise at Morgan's actions.

The ex-wrestler, after walking slowly to the Cadillac's rear while sweeping a searching gaze all around, suddenly began to move with haste. He shot up the trunk lid, grabbed out and put on a garment; it was a sleeveless, thick, quilted jacket that reached his knees. Next he donned a drab topcoat, buttoning it to his chin. He took from the coat's pockets a cap and a pair of spectacles; cap

47

he pulled down to his eyebrows and ears, thick rimless glasses he perched low on his nose.

He slammed down the lid and turned toward the exit.

Lefty shot away from his corner. Racing madly he covered the alley, zagged through moving cars, reached the van and stuck his head inside.

"Coming out now," he gasped. "Walking. And he's changed clothes."

"Changed clothes?"

Lefty darted a look behind. "Here he comes!"

Oliver stared at the man emerging from the alley. He was amazed at the difference. Dave Morgan had changed from a vigorous, heavy man of thirty-odd to a droopy, fat man of late middle age. The cap hid his hair totally, the sides being shaved high. His head was cocked forward and down, enabling him to see over the glasses and at the same time increasing his jowl's girth by their pressing on his collar.

"Clever," said Oliver, impressed. "Damn clever."

"What's it all about though?"

Oliver grinned. He looked almost boyish. "I don't know, not yet. But this is good news, good news."

"Must be up to something, eh?"

"Exactly."

Dave Morgan stepped off the curb and in a sagging flat-footed walk came across the street, passing mere yards ahead of the van. He joined a group of people at a bus stop.

Oliver, who had sunk low in his seat, said, "He doesn't know you. Get on the bus with him. I'll be behind."

Lefty sauntered away. He was in his element. Lighting a cigarette in finest on-camera style he moved in and around the waiting people and Morgan.

A bus came. Dave Morgan got on board. Flicking away his cigarette, shrugging and glaring an unnecessary warning at Oliver, Lefty followed.

There were no free seats. Lefty stood two people from the ex-wrestler, whom he heard ask for a twenty-cent ticket. Lefty bought the same. Ten minutes passed.

The driver gave one of his unintelligible shouts. Morgan turned. Lefty retreated and was first off the bus when it stopped. He found himself in a semi-slum district.

Dave Morgan alighted and slap-footed his way along to a corner formed by a delicatessen, where he turned into a broad street lined with tenement houses. Many a window held a card claiming fine rooms to let. Shrieking children were playing baseball.

From the corner, Lefty watched Dave Morgan slump across the road and enter a house. Oliver drew up, was told the situation, continued on along the main street and parked.

During the following twenty minutes Lefty Steel hung around the store, sent "no action" signals to Oliver and alternated between Eddie Constantine and Sheldon Leonard.

At last the ex-wrestler stepped out into the street.

Half an hour later Oliver and Lefty were back at the corner store after following Dave Morgan to the Cadillac —where he changed clothes—and following the Cadillac until it was obvious that the goal was Marlake, that the morning's activities were over.

Oliver stopped the panel truck and switched off. "Wait here. I'll handle this. Number twenty-four, did you say?"

He got out, rounded the corner and crossed to number twenty-four, whose dim hallway was open to the street. On the first door inside was chalked *Landlady Knock Loud.* He knocked loud.

The door was opened by a man with an unpleasant face who snapped, "So?"

Oliver put his charm to work. Smiling, roughening his accent, he said to the forty-ish man, "Mornin', young fella. I wonder if you'd tell me where I'd find a drinkin' buddy of mine. Got a tip for him on the three o'clock. We calls him Jumbo. Don't know his real name." He added, his tone endowing the other with great understanding, "You know how it is."

The man produced a milder expression. "Jumbo?"

"Yeah, that's it."

"Big? Fifty or sixty?"

"You got it. Wears specs and a cap. Moved in here recent like."

"Dan Mitchell. Five weeks ago. Couldn't be anyone else. He's got number eight. Back room near the bathroom."

"Thanks, son. I'll pop up and see him."

"Out. Just saw him leave."

Oliver displayed disappointment. "That's a bugger that is."

"Missed him by half an hour."

"Well, what time's he get back?"

"Dunno. Works on trains. Odd hours. Goes to Halifax and back, stuff like that."

"Is there any special time or day I could catch him home?"

"Not so far as I know."

"Does he have a day off?"

The man shrugged. "Dunno."

Oliver found he was reluctant to pry further—a reluctance that stemmed from his not wanting to queer another man's pitch, which, he concluded with amusement, was rather odd under the circumstances.

"Anyway," the landlord said, "he'll be keeping more regular hours soon. He's gonna change jobs."

"Yeah?" Oliver said. "How soon?"

"Soon. That's all he said. Real soon."

Oliver backed to the door. He had learned enough. "Well, maybe with his new job he'll shave off that great ginger tash of his."

The man shook his head. "Got no mustache."

"No? Can't be Jumbo then. This *is* number forty-two?"

"Twenty-four. You got the wrong place."

With a joke about his stupidity, Oliver left. He thought: Real soon.

It was the noon rush in Mortimer's Billiards Emporium. All tables were occupied. The hall was crowded with men in business suits and boiler suits and shabby suits, youths in school uniforms and oil-stained aprons and slick jackets.

Some played, some waited to play, most watched and others were interested mainly in the lunches they had brought. The background music was a comforting murmur of voices interspersed with the clean click of ivory.

Mr. Mortimer poured tea, served sandwiches, reckoned charges, added names to the waiting list and hummed *Lili of Laguna*.

When a break came in the work he noticed the tune he was humming. He stopped himself. This had happened three times already today. He couldn't imagine why the tune kept coming back, or why it had come in the first place.

He took up his favorite lean on the counter, looking about with satisfaction. As he looked, it occurred to him what a wonderfully democratic machine was a poolhall. Its users were unaided or unhindered by their lack of or possession of status, background, education, calling. The common denominator was a man's ability with a cue. Bank managers showed the greatest respect for insolvents in jeans and lawyers bowed to inarticulate debt dodgers. A man who outside might slouch, could here, if skilled, square his shoulders in the friendly gloom and feel himself the peer of anyone.

The idea pleased Mr. Mortimer. Utopian. He was, he thought, doing his liberal bit to abrogate false values. And with the Billiards Palace 50 Tables 50 his bit would be multiplied tenfold. He was a public servant, in the purest sense.

Smiling at the future, he began to hum *Lili of Laguna*. After two bars he once again broke off. For no particular reason, or so he thought, he turned his mind to Mrs. Chaps the char.

Mrs. Chaps was a fine person. He was glad he had told her about his dreams. She had understood perfectly how much it meant to him. She was, in fact, a very understanding woman. Charming too. Comfortable. Attractive. A fine woman altogether. And wasn't it curious that she hadn't asked for the new hourly rate which all other local cleaning women were now getting? Faithful, that was Mrs. Chaps.

Mr. Mortimer resolved to offer her the new rate tomorrow—no, not offer, make her accept it.

Redly smiling with pride and nervousness at his generosity, he started once more to hum.

This time when he fell silent it was caused not from within but without: Lefty Steel had entered.

Mr. Mortimer watched warily as the pimply young man threaded his way through the crowd, taking the longest route and looking about him constantly as though suspicious of having his pocket picked.

Lefty came in a final gliding sidle to the counter, leaned close, cupped a hand beside his mouth and said, "Phone Erik. We meet here later in the quiet time. Okay?"

"Yes."

Lefty nodded, slanted his eyes, sidled off.

The big smile Jonesy had been wearing to usher out the customer who had spent three dollars fell away when the green panel truck rattled to a stop outside. Jonesy was fed up. Oliver lousy Jet living for free was bad enough, borrowing guy's vans all the time was going too far. And not only that, this waiting was too much. The con deal was lasting forever, not that there'd be a mountain of dough when it did come off, and if the fuzz stepped in it could mean stir for all.

Jonesy folded his arms. He decided to be firm, find out when this mysterious swindle was going to be finished, exactly what it was and how dangerous it was.

Oliver came in. He glanced sharply at Jonesy and, instead of pushing it to behind him, turned to close the door to give himself thinking time. He could see what was coming.

Jonesy asked bluntly, "When you gonna get to the end of this caper?"

There was, Oliver thought as he turned, only one way to deal with this—attack. He put his hands in his pockets and frowned. "Why?"

"Because I want to know. It's costing me good money

to keep you going. I can't do it indefinitely. And if your caper's too risky you can think of something else."

"I see," Oliver said. "If that's the way you feel, there's only one thing to do."

"Which is?" Jonesy asked, not sure of himself now due to the other's attitude.

"We'll terminate our association. I'll move out, and when the kill comes off I'll send the trifling amount I owe you."

Feeling a lot less sure of himself, Jonesy let his arms fall and mumbled.

Oliver chased with a freezing tone. "If you think that I, who have earned millions, who have worked with the best men in the world, who have pulled some of the biggest capers of all time, if you think I am going to be dictated to by you—you're crazy."

"Well . . ."

"I'll leave this afternoon."

Jonesy thought quickly. This was either where he lost money and risk, or took a chance on both. He decided the last was best. After all, Oliver *was* Oliver Jet. And a quarter of the money needn't be the limit.

He was about to speak when the stairway door opened.

Pel came in. She paused, looking from one man to the other, before asking Jonesy if he had any sugar. He gave her a packet.

Momentarily Oliver forgot his worry of being homeless when he saw the hands of the others seem to linger together as the packet was exchanged.

Pel left the shop.

"Er, look, Oliver," Jonesy said. "Don't take me the wrong way. I was just a bit worried. You know? Anything you do is all right with me. So let's not have any talk of leaving."

"Very well. But let's not have any more questions."

"It's a deal."

At the stairs Oliver said, "By the way, I'm running short on cash."

"Sure, Oliver, sure. Here, take a fin."

With an expression of distaste Oliver tucked the five dollars into his breast pocket. "See you later."

"Yeah, see you."

They separated, each letting out a sigh at what a close thing that had been.

In the kitchen, Pel looked up from her work when Oliver appeared in the doorway. "Hi," she said. "What was going on down there between you two?"

Oliver said, "I should be asking that question."

She looked at him in surprise. "What d'you mean?"

"What was going on down there between you two?— that question. I saw the way you tickled fingers."

Pel's face screwed up with puzzlement. "Tickled fingers?"

"You know what I'm talking about."

She laughed. "I didn't know you were jealous of Jonesy."

"Of course I'm not," Oliver said stiffly. "He's too ugly. I simply thought that if anything was going on I ought to know about it."

"Ah, knock it off, honey. There's nothing going on and you know there isn't."

He turned away, went to the bedroom.

Pel shook her head at Oliver's behavior and as she returned to the food began to think about Jonesy.

If the finger bit had been deliberate, it was real stupid. How old did he think she was? They used to do that sort of jazz at school, tickling the palm of your hand and asking, "Know what that means?" If he thought kid stuff like that would get him anywhere he was wrong. He must be a jerk. But he wasn't ugly, like Oliver said. Not handsome either. He was sort of cute. And after all, there must be something to him if Oliver was jealous.

The Great Erik combed his precise hair, adjusted his eye patch and looked at his watch. It was getting close to the time when he would be suitably a little late for the meeting at Mr. Mortimer's. He left his room and went out of the boardinghouse.

54

Walking toward town, Erik reflected with annoyance on the outcome of his bruncheon date with Miranda. They had parted coldly, for the jealousy he had feigned had led at last to sharp words. His annoyance was directed purely at himself. He had overdone the act and then had failed to understand her inevitable, natural crossness.

Now, with a hurt twist of his neck in his collar, Erik admitted that he had not been putting on an act. True jealousy had been the cause of his harping. *Had* Miranda gone further with Morgan than she had said? The thought brought an actual pain in his stomach—like those pains he used to get on the rare occasions when his mother, amazingly, hadn't let him have his own way. He knew he was being foolish, that Miranda's past affairs were none of his business. Nowadays a woman didn't stay virginal for long, which was quite right. The hell it was. Erik's pain increased as he wished, fervently, clenching his hands, as he had often wished before, that Miranda had been innocent when they met.

At the first flower shop he ordered a dozen red roses sent along with his card to Miranda. The salesgirl gushed and Erik felt grand. His pain went.

Heading for Waterloo Street, Erik mused on the why of this meeting. It could only mean that Oliver Jet had got onto something through following Dave Morgan. No doubt Jet would make the most of his story—after, of course, he had finally arrived. But this time he might be the one to be first for a change.

Erik looked at his watch and slowed down.

When he entered the poolhall ten dawdled minutes later he sighed on finding there only the proprietor and Lefty Steel. He was still greeting them when the swing doors twanged and in came Oliver Jet.

Although put out that the con man somehow always managed to upstage him, Erik couldn't help but admire Oliver for it and for his general assertion of presence, his sound sense of Theatre. He watched appreciatively as Oliver strolled up the hall, gave each man a nod, moved to the counter end and elegantly lighted a cigarette.

"Well?" blurted Mr. Mortimer.

Oliver blew out smoke. "Gentlemen, if we are going to move at all, we've got to move quickly."

After allowing the silence that followed to have its moment, while Mr. Mortimer fingered his mustache and Erik stopped thinking how another time he could hide outside until the con man had entered, Oliver said:

"Tell them the first part, Lefty."

Standing tall with importance the younger man told of trailing Dave Morgan to outer Hamilton, the change of appearance, the bus ride, the lodging house.

He was disappointed when, instead of offering congratulations or at least looking impressed, Mr. Mortimer and the Great Erik merely turned back to Oliver Jet, who said:

"Our friend of the muscles has created another identity for himself. Dan Mitchell, a man who works odd hours on the railroad. Morgan's been smart about it, apart from his excellent disguise, not going to the new place only on his day off but any old time, letting himself be seen there if only for ten minutes. He'll be perfectly safe with his story of a change of job when he's there permanently. No one will connect him with youngish Dave Morgan, who's run off from Marlake with a fortune."

Erik said, "Which must, of course, be the reason for all this."

"Without a doubt."

"Well!" exclaimed Mr. Mortimer.

"Didn't take us long to get something on Morgan, did it?" asked Lefty, grinning. His grin dropped when Oliver said, "That is not the point."

"No?"

"I'm afraid not. I can't see any way of using this against him. If we threaten exposure he'll simply call it off or use some other method, perhaps a fake robbery. And his exposure wouldn't do *us* any good. No, all we can do is beat him to it."

Mr. Mortimer drummed his fingers. "Why did you say we've got to move quickly?"

"His change of job. It will be soon, any day now."

The four men exchanged glances. It seemed there was nothing to be said. They were back at the familiar fumbling stage.

Silence.

"Er . . ." Mr. Mortimer began, and changed to a good clearing of his throat.

"Yeah," said Lefty, after which he offered a cigarette to Erik, had the offer declined and returned the pack to his pocket.

Silence.

Oliver tutted with impatience, thinking of the professionals he knew and with whom he might have become involved for his fall to robbery in preference to this bunch of babies.

"One thing," Erik said. "Morgan's plan shows the safeful of money's not a tall story."

"Yes it does," Mr. Mortimer agreed eagerly. "It certainly does."

"Yeah," said Lefty Steel.

Silence.

"We're making great progress," Oliver said.

Erik shot him a hard look. "Have you any ideas?" He was mortified by the confidence man replying with a bland, "Yes."

Oliver got out his cigarettes to gain time in thinking of a follow-up to his lie. He thought of one, to his surprise, while waving out a match.

"Yes," he said. "I believe it's time that the Great Erik did, or tried to do, what he was initially brought into this affair for. Namely, the squaring of Dave Morgan."

Erik said, "He's not about to play."

"After all," Oliver went on, "we've all done our bit. Following people, watching houses, asking questions. Getting ourselves well implicated."

Erik's manner was cold. "I'm implicated too. I pumped Morgan. That's why we're stuck—remember?"

"But that's really all you've done, you know," ventured Mr. Mortimer with reluctance.

Erik turned on him. "And what did you do that was so bloody special?"

Oliver held up a hand. "Let's not have any backbiting, gentlemen. If Erik doesn't want to help find a way to the money . . ." He shrugged.

Erik said, "I can't see him co-operating, can you? Especially now. There's no reason why he should."

"You might be able to do it anyway," murmured Mr. Mortimer. "You never know till you try."

"All right," Erik snapped. "I'll try. If, that is, someone will be so good as to tell me how I get hold of the man."

Oliver became brisk. "Simple. Lefty will wait outside Mrs. Vandle's. Right now. There's no time to lose. If Morgan goes out for a drink Lefty can tail him and phone you when he settles." He added, "Lefty's very good at that sort of thing."

The younger man, who had been thinking with a scowl that he was sick of all this waiting about at Mrs. Vandle's, stopped thinking so, stopped scowling, and smiled.

"Soon as I've checked in at work," he said, "I'll go along and really watch that house."

Erik said, "You don't have a car."

Mr. Mortimer said, "He can use my bicycle."

Oliver said, "If Morgan wants a drink, there're only five or six places to go. Lefty can find him."

Lefty said, "Don't worry, that Morgan won't give me the slip."

Erik nodded. "Fine, so long as I'm not onstage at the time." He looked at the confidence man. "Now how about you going to see Morgan's stand-in, the retired matron?" Expecting an argument, he was again nonplused, for Oliver gave an airy, assenting shrug.

"Very well," he said.

"Go to her house," insisted Erik. "Sound her out."

"Quite."

"Right now. There's no time to lose."

"Of course."

"Well then," said Erik sulkily.

Outside, walking along Waterloo Street, Oliver fumed at himself for playing it so big. He could have declined, said that a job like wrapping up the matron would take weeks, considering it to be at all possible. He could have said a lot of things. But that would have made him as small and quibbly as the Great Twit. Impossible thought.

Erik was already turning onto the lakefront, having narrowly beaten Oliver Jet into making the first exit, which tiny triumph had made him feel better about his enforced assignment. In any case, he mused, it was not going to be without interest, and there were enough obstacles to success to render failure acceptable.

Mr. Mortimer hummed broken, nervous snatches of *Lili of Laguna* while putting tea leaves in the urn and thinking badly of the traitorous Dave Morgan.

Into the Kwik Kar Wash stalked Humphrey Bogart, who crumpled at once into Lefty Steel when a voice bellowed, "You're fired!"

Dave Morgan, alias Dan Mitchell, alias David Goliath, wearing coveralls and high rubber boots, turned the faucet to bring surging sensuous life to the hose. Wavingly he sprayed the Cadillac, gripping the hose tip to make a skinny jet.

He worked slowly—there was so little to do at Mrs. Vandle's—and as he worked allowed his mind to wander over the details of the plan which he had evolved after much careful thought.

Roughly once a month Mrs. Vandle announced that she wished to be left undisturbed for the evening as she intended checking her money and valuables: announced with an aloof importance which hinted at senility. There was no evidence that she looked in her safe at any other time. Almost four weeks having passed since the last check, the next would fall any day now. The night following would be the time for action. Mrs. Vandle would have a sedative slipped into her bedtime cocoa, later the key would be taken from around her neck, the safe emptied and the key returned. The next morning, after asking permission to visit his parents in Toronto, he would leave with his disguise, take a train to Hamilton and change his appearance on the way. He would telephone back to say his father was ill and wanted him to stay on for a few days, and the calls could continue during the following weeks to allay suspicion until the next safe-checking, by which time he would be firmly established in his new personality and have eased some aspects of disguise, letting his weight balloon, as it so easily did, and changing his hair.

Dave Morgan smiled. He sprayed the car with generous sweeps of the hose. Everything, he thought, was going to be golden. After a suitable time, maybe a year, he'd get a passport in some name and go abroad. He'd be set for life. He'd have lots of money, and . . . well, he'd have lots of money.

Wealth. The thought filled him with a tingle, which grew steadily stronger as he pictured himself surrounded by dollar bills.

He is up to his knees in cash. He wades around in circles. He stuffs handfuls of the green darlings into every pocket, down his socks, under his shirt, inside his pants. He flops down, swoops up his hands and lets the money patter on his head.

The tingle in Morgan rose to a gorgeous crescendo. His smile broke out into a short foolish spluttery laugh and his hand opened on the hose so that the water went *splat!*

The retired hospital matron, a Miss Farmer, lived at number nine. Oliver Jet had walked past number nine so often in the past half hour that he was nervous of repeating the act. It was nervousness that had made him walk past in the first instance, instead of going to the door. His courage had failed him every time.

Why?—he asked himself angrily as he stood on the street corner. Why the hesitation? Why didn't he simply go to the door, summon Miss Farmer, smile and say . . . what?

He seethed at himself. There were dozens of things to say. Hundreds. For instance he could murmur, the smile shy, "Good evening, Miss Farmer. My name's Tom Smith."

"Yes?"

"I saw you the other day in town and took the liberty of finding out your name and address."

"Really?"—frowning.

"I should explain, before you begin to think me a madman, that I'm an artist."

The frown goes, she relaxes. "I see."

"You may have heard of me. Tom Smith."

"Yes, there does seem to be something familiar about the name."

"The point is, Miss Farmer, I saw you and was struck instantly by your face, its strength, character, perfect bone structure."

She smiles and blushes. "Would you care to step inside?"

Yes, it could be as easy as that. Get in with any kind of flattering nonsense. In the old days there had been many times when his approach was nonsensical, for the hell of it, to test his powers or another's gullibility. Nothing to it.

Oliver marched along to the gate of number nine. He didn't hesitate. Pushing through he walked to the door and knocked a firm tattoo. There was no wait: the door swung inward almost before the knock's echo had died.

Miss Farmer was tall, stout, and sixty, with a hawk-like face and white hair cut as short as a man's. Looking coldly at Oliver she asked, "Well?"

He let out a breath he had not known he was holding. Dully, sadly, he heard himself ask, "Could you tell me the right time, please?"

She snapped a glance at her wrist watch. "Nearly seven."

"Thank you." He was suddenly aware that his heart was beating at far above the normal rate.

Miss Farmer frowned. "Didn't I see you walk by the house? Twice, in fact?"

"No," Oliver said, backing away. "Er, yes, actually you did, come to think of it. I was lost."

She made no answer.

He turned, passed through the gateway and went shakily up the street. The moment he judged himself to be out of Miss Farmer's sight he changed to a fast march.

His mind gabbled questions: Will she phone the cops? Why ask the time? Will she tell Morgan, tell it as something funny, and will he recognize the description? Why not the artist bit? Was she phoning the cops right now? Had she already? Were they on their way?

He answered every question satisfactorily, calmingly— and then broke into a run.

He ran to the corner, across a main road and into an area of streets narrow and winding. He stopped at last because of staring people, making a play of looking at his watch and shaking his head.

Walking, struggling with his breath, he felt a fool for the run. It was quite unnecessary, he thought, there was no danger. It was the result of nerves. Asking the time had been the right thing to do. Months would be needed to get even a pleasant word out of an old bitch like Miss Farmer.

He spotted a beer parlor. As he headed for it he recalled his date to meet Jonesy and Pel later at the Hotel Waterloo. He also recalled Pel.

Forgetting his apologia of a minute before, he told himself that whatever happened he still had Pel, there was always Pel.

The bullet from the G-man's gun hit him in the lower belly. He doubled, clutched the wound, staggered forward. His breathing came harsh and fast. The pain was terrible, but he, he could stand it. Not many could, but he could. He wouldn't beg for mercy or help. He would die the way he had lived, defiantly, sneering. Another bullet tore through his arm, another slashed across his cheek, another shattered . . .

A car went by. Lefty Steel straightened quickly and saw Dave Morgan at the wheel of the brown Cadillac. Flushed

62

from playing Cornered Hood, and disappointed that the game was over, Lefty reached boredly for Mr. Mortimer's bicycle.

A large crowd, mostly tourist, sat drinking in the Hotel Waterloo. The air was feculent and the people loud.

Pel was having a marvelous time. She liked people and she liked noise. Jonesy had bought her three drinks and and told her a score of dirty jokes. The drinks were great and the jokes fantastic. She'd been in tears half a dozen times. He was the funniest man she had ever met in her whole entire life. He kept trying to get fresh, of course, but she could handle that.

Jonesy said, "Here comes your young man." He emphasized the adjective.

Pel ignored him and smiled toward Oliver while blinking to remove the haze from her eyes. She thought how handsome Ollie was. She really liked Ollie. He was mature and smart. She liked the way he now kissed her cheek before sitting at her side, and the highfalutin way he began to talk to Jonesy, and how neatly he cut him off in the middle of a joke to tell of a funny incident on one of his past capers. It was an amusing story. It just went on a bit long, that's all. But very amusing.

Oliver told another anecdote. When he started on a third, again cutting into his host's efforts, Pel began to feel a shade sorry for Jonesy. She furthermore began to feel superior. Oliver was working so hard to entertain her and hold her attention, and was so obviously delighted at succeeding, that in her scale of values she rose somewhat while he sank.

Pel leaned back to allow Jonesy a better position and smiled mysteriously at the ceiling.

"And now, ladies and gentlemen," said the comedy team straight man, who introduced some of the acts, "the star of our show, the man you've all been waiting for, one of the world's greatest exponents of the art of illusion, the Great Erik!"

63

The meager audience produced a reasonable round of applause.

Erik, wearing white tie and tails, top hat and eye patch, strolled onto the stage. He went into his act, taking it at a leisurely pace. This half hour was his own and he lived every minute of it to the fullest. When onstage he knew that everything in the past had been worthwhile—his struggles, his lean years, his mother's sacrifices.

Tonight he felt happier than usual, for he and Miranda had played a romantic scene on the catwalk and made up for their tiff. He knew he had been a fool to be jealous.

Miming, he performed trick after trick, using only playing cards, short lengths of rope and cigars. The response was good. When he was returning to the stage after having produced eggs from the ears of people in the front rows, he caught a signal from the wings: telephone. Gesturing that the caller should hold on, Erik hurried the act to a close.

He took two curtains, went across to the wall telephone and lifted the dangling receiver. As expected, the caller was Lefty Steel. He reported that Dave Morgan was having a drink in the lounge of the Chieftain Hotel.

Ten minutes later, having told Miranda he had to make a call about his grandfather, Erik was on his way. He had removed his make-up and wore a topcoat over his stage clothes.

Though dark now, Lakeshore Drive was ablaze with lights. The amusements boomed music, the crowd moved thickly. Erik was gratified to receive countless glances of recognition. He was further gratified by the fact that this made him realize it would be better to dispense with the eye patch if he was to be seen with Dave Morgan.

He reached the hotel and took off his patch as he went in. Still more satisfaction came when he entered the cocktail lounge: Morgan was not only still here but alone, and not only alone but isolated, standing at one end of the long bar while most of the other customers were gathered at the near end.

Morgan was faced away, looking out of the picture window which gave onto the lake.

Erik went by the ex-wrestler and moved to the bar. "Hello, Dave," he said casually.

Morgan started. He grunted a reply and drew back his head to look at Erik with suspicion.

Erik said, "I just came out for a drink after the show." Which, he thought, was a pretty damn vacuous thing to say.

Dave Morgan picked up and drained his glass. He appeared to be on the point of leaving.

"Good house tonight," Erik went on, still casual, examining the change he had brought from his pocket. "There's life in vaudeville yet. Brandy and ginger ale, please."

The suspicion in Morgan's eyes faltered. He seemed less eager to go. The scoring agents, Erik knew, were his attitude, the fact that he hadn't offered to buy a drink and Morgan's desire to talk shop.

"Yes," Erik said, "music hall isn't dead by any means. There'll always be a place for top performers."

"I think you're right."

"I was saying so last night to Watson, the producer. You know Watson, don't you, Dave?"

"Sure."

Erik talked on. Morgan appeared to relax. He leaned against the bar, and when Erik's drink came ordered another ale for himself. Soon he was cheerfully exchanging views on artistes, on gossip, on show business in general.

While talking, Erik had been toying with various ways of getting around to the hot point. One outshone the others. It not only introduced the subject of money, it was concerned with an idea which must surely grab Dave Morgan in the tenderest part of his soul.

Gesturing to the bartender to do the drinks again, Erik said, "Of course, the biggest thing in Canadian live theater today is wrestling."

Morgan nodded vigorously. "You can say that again."

65

He went on to tell of the size of recent gates in the East and what television was paying.

"Yes," Erik said, "there's a fortune to be made for the right people, the ones who know both the technical side and the theatrical side—what gimmicks to use, how to build up a promotion."

"I guess so."

"As a matter of fact, Dave, a promoter friend of mine and I are going to do just that."

"Is that right?"

Erik looked thoughtfully into his glass. "You know, it's just occurred to me that you, Dave, might be the man we've been looking for. We were going to approach Whipper Wilson, but he's getting on now. The thing is, we want an actual wrestler in the partnership."

Raising his eyes, Erik saw that Morgan was watching him keenly. Erik pushed home the clincher. "We're putting in fifty thousand each. Could you swing that much?"

Morgan laughed. "You must be kidding. Me? I earn three hundred a month, plus keep."

"But there must be some way you could raise the money."

Morgan smiled. "How?"

Erik looked at him steadily. "There are ways, Dave."

Morgan lifted his full glass of beer and emptied it in four swallows. He ballooned his cheeks, popped out a belch and said, "The only way I'll ever get money is to find me a rich broad."

They both laughed.

Two minutes later they had become bitter enemies.

Erik began the loathing with a question not of his conscious volition. He was astonished to hear himself ask:

"Seen Miranda lately?"

Morgan cocked his head. "Eh?"

"Er, about this money."

"Miranda, did you say?"

"You know, my fiancée," Erik said, hating himself. "I—um—wondered if you'd seen her around."

Morgan shrugged. "Why should I? I hardly know her."

66

Erik shifted his neck in his collar, furious both with himself and the strong man. "Come now. You know her quite well. Don't be dense."

Morgan eased back. A spot of color appeared on either cheek. In a quiet voice he said, "Don't call me dense."

Erik spoke quickly: "Sorry, Dave. No offense. Now about this money. But you have been out with Miranda so don't talk like a fool. Fifty thousand dollars. She's engaged to me and—"

"Don't," Morgan said, leaning forward and putting a forefinger on Erik's chest, "call me dense and don't call me no goddamn fools." His face was fully flushed.

Erik's was also flushed. He could have killed himself. He gave a self-order to take it easy. Instead, he brushed the other's hand away with a sneered, "Let's not get physical."

"Me? With a dwarf like you? I'd be ashamed."

"You son-of-a-bitch," hissed Erik, frightened and angry and still astonished at himself. He was trembling.

The people at the far end of the bar had turned to watch.

Dave Morgan took hold of Erik's lapel. "Listen, dwarf bastard, think yourself lucky that I don't pick on children. But I can be pushed too far. So do yourself a good turn: stay away from me in future."

"Son-of-a-bitch," mumbled Erik, staring at Morgan's bared teeth, "son-of-a-bitch." His self-hatred increased as his eyes began to mist with tears. "Rotten son-of-a-bitch."

"Shurrup."

"Muscle head, fool, brainless mother—"

The following moment everything in Erik's vision was turned topsy-turvy. Lights flashed, furniture raced, there was a fast pan of eager faces. He felt a hard thudding on his buttocks. Not until he found himself staggering for balance and finding it by grabbing a chair did he realize that he had been off his feet, that in horrifying fact he had been put over Morgan's knee and spanked. Spanked!

Erik gaped in stupefaction after Morgan, who was walking down the lounge, who stopped now to throw back, "Dwarf!"

He stopped again by the door before making his bull-like exit to hurl a final epithet, or, as far as Erik was concerned, the ultimate epithet:

"Cuckold!"

The word exploded in the painful silence. Erik, his body scorched with shame, listened in horror to the word as it played itself over and over in his ears.

Someone giggled.

Erik tried to act naturally. He straightened. His hands went in and out of his pockets. A sick semblance of a smile worked jittery tricks on his lips.

The bartender was poised in the act of polishing a glass. The people were frozenly, delightedly watching. Time had stopped.

The heat of Erik's body was such that he thought he would faint. He forced himself to walk: to go past the silent watchers and out of the lounge.

He was followed by another giggle.

The cool night air outside brought ease. Erik stood with closed eyes. He took a deep, shuddery breath—and knew that Dave Morgan, as a threat to the scheme, had to die.

THREE

It was a blustery gray morning, chill, a broad hint that summer had run its course and that if winter had any say in the matter, Canadian winter with a reputation to uphold, warmth was a dirty word and the following months would be consistently tone on tone gray. However: winter's designs failed to affect the atmosphere of the poolroom, which, daylight or dark, spring or fall, remained true to its policy of apartheid, non-involvement with reality.

Mr. Mortimer was at one end of the hall ironing table five, while at the other Mrs. Chaps stood on tiptoe to gouge a ceiling angle with a long feather duster. Her humming of *Lili of Laguna* made Mr. Mortimer smile. He thought how funny that tunes were so catching. She must have heard him humming the song and now she too had become affected.

A moment later his smile dropped. After its brief vacation, his mind had inevitably returned to Erik's scheme for the success of their plan.

When last night, by summons, the four men had met on the landing outside the swing doors—the hall being full —Erik had followed Oliver Jet's story of a long, fruitless conversation with Miss Farmer with the flat statement that their problem was solved, that Morgan was going to be fixed.

Fixed. An innocent enough word in itself. But next Erik had said:

"Now we need a gun."

No one spoke.

"We need a gun," Erik repeated. "To fix Morgan."

Oliver Jet said quietly that he knew where one could be bought, and asked, "Who's going to do the fixing?"

Erik brought a coin from his pocket. "I suggest we toss for it."

Again no one spoke.

Erik smiled. Mr. Mortimer got the impression that he had expected this result, had hoped for it, wanting for some reason to put his partners down.

"Very well," Erik said. "I'll do it myself. For a consideration."

"What?"

"I want forty per cent of the proceeds."

The others exchanged glances. Oliver Jet said, "We get twenty instead of twenty-five per cent. It's okay by me."

"And me."

"And me."

They went on to make arrangements.

Now Mr. Mortimer thought: Fixed. Gun. Surely that meant . . .

His mind skittered back from the abyss, fearing the drop to truth. But before getting too far back, his mind did produce, hopefully and plaintively, a vision of Dave Morgan being shot in the leg.

Breaking off cloth-ironing, which slow chore permitted too easily the following of thoughts, Mr. Mortimer put away the equipment and turned with relief to Mrs. Chaps.

After they had toyed with local gossip, Mr. Mortimer introduced a serious note with, "Ambition's a funny thing, isn't it?" He was faintly surprised at the question.

"Nothing wrong with ambition," Mrs. Chaps said. "There's nothing better a man could have."

"True, but sometimes it makes people go too far, don't you think?"

"Oh, I don't know."

"I mean, some people'll do desperate things to get what they want, won't they?"

"*Some* people, Mr. Mortimer."

"Oh certainly. Of course. Quite so."

"With decent folk, the means is justified by the end."

He put his head on one side, looking at her with new respect. "The means is . . . Yes, Mrs. Chaps, you are absolutely right. So long as the end is honorable, which is to say worthy."

"And what," she asked, her eyes amused, "could be worthier than the ambition of a certain gentleman what will remain nameless?"

They laughed, happy at sharing a secret, while Mr. Mortimer told himself that the end was worthy all right; democratic, pleasure-giving, a far better use for money than lying in some old safe.

Jovial, he asked, "How about a nice cup of tea, Mrs. Chaps?"

"Lovely, Mr. Mortimer."

At the counter, sipping from a cracked cup, the charwoman murmured, "Good tea. Tasty."

70

"Ah, but it's not the same as a home brew, Mrs. Chaps."

"I must say, I don't think you can get the same flavor in these big urns as you can in a pot."

"Are you India or Ceylon?"

"Ceylon."

"Me too. One spoon per, and one for the pot?"

"Exactly."

"Pottery or metal?"

"Oh, pottery. You can't beat a good china teapot I always say. My mother was pottery too."

"Tea cozy?"

"Of course," said Mrs. Chaps, wriggling back her chin. "Naturally."

Mr. Mortimer nodded with satisfaction. "I might have known."

Their eyes smiled as their mouths sipped. Now they not only shared a secret but also an appreciation of life's finer things.

"Yes," Mrs. Chaps said, "I've never approved of mashing tea on the flame."

"I'll bet you make a very decent brew, Mrs. Chaps."

"Well, I've never had no complaints, Mr. Mortimer."

"I'm sure you haven't, Mrs. Chaps."

Of a sudden, they were both stiff and formal.

Flushing, the char said mumblingly, running her words together, "You're welcome to come and take a cup with me any time you like."

"This afternoon," he said promptly.

"Four-thirty," she said. "Thirty Lime Street."

Without another word they separated. Mrs. Chaps hurried back to her work and Mr. Mortimer made himself over-busy at the sink.

Jonesy turned from his doughnut machine. The slowness of business all morning, combined with the fact that he had let himself be conned into loaning Oliver Jet twenty dollars, decided him it was time he had another talk with Pel, put to her the idea that had been growing stronger in the past two days.

Upstairs in the living room he called, "Pel?"

She wandered in from a bedroom, holding a dressing gown closed.

"Not dressed yet?" he asked. "It's nearly noon."

"Been taking a bath. The water wasn't very hot."

Swallowing a retort for the complaint, Jonesy said, "We had a nice time last night, didn't we?"

Pel smiled. "Yes, we did."

"Until Ollie showed up."

"Now now." She wagged a playfully reproving finger as she moved across the room.

Watching Pel sway to the couch and sit, Jonesy wondered if she was wearing anything under that robe.

Not wearing anything under her robe, Pel wondered if it was sensible to be around Jonesy. But her body felt so fine. She felt fine altogether after the bath. Relaxed. Smooth. Cuddly. Funny things, baths.

"I mean it," Jonesy said. "And I'm not being nasty. It was great till he showed up."

"What did poor Ollie do?"

"You know, those stories of his. I must say, it's real good of you to put up with 'em, Pel. Kind."

"Oh well." She lay down on the couch and clasped both hands behind her head. "Did you want to talk to me, Jonesy?"

"I did, yeah," he said, raising his eyebrows at her actions. "Confidential business."

She stretched comfortably. "Mmmm?"

Jonesy crossed the room. Actions, he told himself. Leave the words till later. She's warm. "Mind if I sit down a minute?"

"I guess not," she said, shifting her hips over.

He sat. "Pel," he said in a low tone, "you're really beautiful. You really are."

I can stop him any time I want to. "Thanks."

Straddling Pel's upper body with his arms Jonesy leaned forward. "Shall I tell you something?"

"Go ahead."

"I got a yen for you."

72

"That right?"

"Yeah."

She could see that he was going to try for a kiss, and as he began to lean closer, she thought she might, there was no harm in it and him being so crazy about her it was a shame not to let him have a bit of a kiss and he could be stopped before he went too far.

Their lips met.

Jubilantly, Jonesy put all he knew of creative sensuality into the act, shaping his mouth, gently rocking his head, exploring with the tip of his tongue. Concentrating on style, he was emotionally detached.

Although she kept her hands behind her head and her teeth closed, Pel allowed her lips to return the pressure. It occurred to her that this was like being a captive, hands tied back, lying at a ravisher's mercy. She began to feel a flicker of excitement.

The kiss went on.

Jonesy slid his right arm down. His hand found its way through the robe and came to Pel's lower thigh, where it rested. For a full half minute the hand was still.

Pel parted her teeth.

Not yet involved, even bored as far as the kiss was concerned, Jonesy moved his hand, put it between Pel's legs.

When Pel had finished being a beautiful young virgin, tied down to be raped by the handsome enemy officer, she thought she would let Jonesy get just so far and no further. As long as nothing serious happened, there was no harm in all this.

Jonesy's hand worked slowly up between legs that were close together yet not too close together. He knew now that he had won. He started to get interested.

Pel sighed shudderingly through her nose, senses focused on the twining tongues and groping hand. There was no harm in it. She would tell him to stop at the last minute.

The last minute arrived. Jonesy's hand came firmly and actively into place. Pel freed her mouth to speak and said, "Don't stop."

Marlake Park is nothing more than an extra large town square. An acre in area, lying two blocks back from the lakeshore and two off the main street, it is looked at by the seedier stores, touristic enterprises, and a car lot. Within a railing are flower beds, trees, and lawns. In the center, where all paths meet, a memorial to the forty young men of Marlake who died in the 1914–18 war has been three-parts obscured by a public convenience, erected by the chamber of commerce to serve the tourists. The building has an exterior of natural wood to strike a rustic note, an interior of glazed tile to discourage the poetic.

Erik, minus his eye patch, walked once around and twice through the park. He circled the lavatory, examining the facing businesses. He noted how many people used the gravel paths and how many were on the sidewalks. He concluded that his choice of murder scene was perfect.

Leaving the park he crossed to one of the long side rows of buildings. Fragilely splitting the row was an alley. Erik entered. He examined the walls on either side. No, there was no lighting: the alley would be dim. Perfect again.

He came to a junction; two alleys splitting the block into quarters. Erik nodded approval. There would be three ways he could go.

Turning right, lakeward, he came out onto a street. From here it was two blocks to Waterloo Street, and the Grand. All perfect.

But Erik did not smile, even slightly. Nothing affected his depression born of suppressed rage and the pain in his stomach, the gnaw which had doubled in strength after hearing on the telephone what he had expected and dreaded to hear.

He had called every hotel and nearly every motel before hitting the right place, with the same story of:

"Look, I lost a photo that's got sentimental value and I'm offering a reward. I think it was in your place but I'm not sure. I was there with a girl, and to tell the God's truth I was using a phony name. You know how it is. Maybe you recall me. I'm tall, pretty heavy, and I've got a crewcut. I drive a brown Caddy."

At last he heard, "Oh sure. With the blonde."

Erik turned leadenly and headed for the repair shop to pick up his car.

The menopausal green van, hot and quivering, lurched off the main road in Toronto with a final flush of power and came to an irritable, exhausted halt. The nearby house, which was new and expensive, seemed to glare at the panel truck for its impertinence.

Oliver Jet switched off the motor. He slumped down, resting his head against the seat. His face was grave and he looked tired: he was worried and he had slept badly.

Murder. He was participating in a murder. The thought was incredible yet true. It had kept him awake, was a lump in his chest. He had several times come close to calling the whole thing off, backing out. And he knew that if he began to think deeply about it now, back out he would. Which would mean his finish. He had to go through with it because he had to have money because he had to have Pel because she was the only thing he had.

But murder . . .

He cut the thought off. It might never come to that. In fact it probably would not. Murder was something which happened to other people, something you read about in newspapers. It had no part in the life of Oliver Jet.

Heavy in face, body, heart, he got from the van and went to the house. His knock was answered by a man his own age wearing a pajama jacket over a shirt and leaning on a stick, a man with impossibly Semitic features, nose too big for his face, tongue too big for his mouth.

"Christ Almighty," he laughed. "The boy himself!"

Oliver forced a grinning, "Harry!"

His hand was shaken, he was urged inside, introduced to a fat wife and ushered into a chair at a table cluttered with the remains of a meal. Beer was served. They talked.

Was Little Charlie still inside? What ever became of Leaping Lena? Shame about Max. Did Minnie Short-time get over her dose? That Sarnia bank job was a honey. Heard the latest on Old Perce? Gelt was scarce. Times had changed. Old days.

At length, regretfully, Oliver looked at his watch. "I don't have a lot of time, Harry."

"Get lost," Harry told his wife, who at once took herself cheerfully away. "Now, Ollie, what can I do for you? Shirts maybe? I got some silks."

"A gun," Oliver said, all casual, looking around the room.

"A gun, eh? What would you want with a gun, Ollie?"

Oliver sighed. "Nothing, believe me. It's for a friend. I owe him a favor. I hate getting involved in these transactions, but a favor is a favor."

"That's the way it goes, Ollie," Harry said, stumping to a closet. "German automatic do? It's all I got."

"Oh, I guess so."

Returning, Harry put down a chocolate box. Oliver looked inside briefly at the gun and its spare clip of ammunition. "How much?"

"Sixty dollars to you."

"Far too cheap. I'll give you eighty."

Harry sat, shaking his head and smiling. "What a character."

Oliver brought out bills and tossed them on the table. "There's twenty on account. I'll drop by to give you the rest soon, when I get back from Boston. I'm flying over tonight on a bit of business."

Harry picked up the money. "Well, okay. But I wouldn't do this for no one else, y'know. Cash on the nail I like. You never can tell what's going to happen to people. But it's okay with you, Ollie. Your name's good with me anytime."

Oliver looked down. "Thank you," he said softly.

In the apartment above Jonesy's store, Pel, wearing slacks and sweater, sat at the table reading a magazine. About what had happened she felt nothing. She had enjoyed the act, was satisfied, and now began to forget as she might forget a meal. The ethics of the matter troubled her in no way—which, had she realized it, would have caused her a twinge of conscience.

Jonesy came into the room. Looking at Pel, he thought, Now.

"So," he mused aloud, "from what Ollie says, the caper's coming to a head. I hope he don't make a mistake. That'd put us all in trouble."

"All?"

"Sure. You and me and Ollie. We'd all be blamed equal."

"And go to jail?"

"Certainly. With Ollie's record we couldn't miss."

"I've got no record."

"Don't matter. We'd all fall."

"Oh," Pel said slowly.

Jonesy thought she had been fed enough of the danger bit. He said, "But I got an idea. It all depends on how you feel about Ollie, like I asked you before."

"I don't know if I love him. He's nice. He's smart. And clever. Look at all the money he's made."

"Them stories you got to take with a block of salt. He never earned nowhere near as much as he says."

"Even so, it's still a lot of money."

"Know what I'd do if I had dough, big dough?"

"Open a chain of shops, I bet."

Jonesy snorted. "Not me. I'd go live in Miami in a upnose hotel. Swim every day, night club every night. Live. That's what I'd do."

Pel smiled broadly. "Sounds great, Jonesy."

"Would you like that too?"

"I'll say. Great."

"Then how'd you like to do it? With me. You and me together."

"There's no use talking like that. You haven't got enough money."

"But I will have. From Ollie."

"Your share's only a quarter. He'd have to get an awful lot."

"What," Jonesy said, "if I got it all?"

She looked at him warily. "How d'you mean?"

"What I mean depends on if you think more of Ollie than of having a ball. And mind this, when he's in the chips he won't want you. He always finds someone to hold his hand when he's down and gives 'em the push when he's up. But you won't want to fool with him anyway, a man that age. He never takes you anyplace. Too old and tired. Me, I'm young. Come in with me, we'll have the time of our lives."

"What did you mean about the money?"

"What if we take all the dough when Ollie gets it? Go over the line? We could buy a car, go anyplace we wanted. How does that sound?"

Feeling uncomfortable, Pel said, "It wouldn't be honest."

"Honesty's got nothing to do with it. It's not honest the way he's getting the dough in the first place."

Pel shrugged.

Jonesy asked, "Now which would be better, living quietly with a man of sixty-odd, never going out, or taking up with a young guy and seeing the world in style, having a ball?"

Pel thought his argument sounded so sensible and right that it seemed stupid not to fall in with his plan at once. Still . . .

"Who d'you like best, Pel?"

"I don't know," she said. She did know, she liked Oliver, but Oliver's idea of real living was on the dull side: he had been talking about a restful vacation in Manitoba.

"Think about it, eh?"

"I will."

"You won't say anything to Ollie?"

"No."

Descending to the store, Jonesy sighed with nervous satisfaction. He felt certain that she was sold on his idea. That high-life line would turn the trick. He wasn't sure he would stay with her after they left with the money, but her help was going to be needed to get it. There might be complications, a check or something. In any case, a couple of weeks together before giving her the slip would be real nice.

It was the quiet time at the poolroom. Only one man, reading a newspaper, was present when Lefty Steel came in to take over as requested. He greeted the proprietor and began to whisper about the scheme, but to his disappointment Mr. Mortimer left hurriedly at the first mention of Oliver Jet's mission.

Jealous, Lefty thought. And Lefty was jealous himself. Buying a gun was really something. It would have been great to go along, hang around silently like a bodyguard. The place would most likely be a regular arsenal, thousands of weapons hidden away in a big room behind something innocent like a flower shop, or maybe in a deserted farm with guards at the gate, and there'd be guys sitting around, planning jobs and stuff. But there was one consolation: he hadn't had to tell about his own gun, and offer its use. He might never have got it back!

The newspaper reader got up and left the hall.

Lefty forgot the caper on realizing that he was alone, beautifully alone, in sole charge of the poolroom.

He stalked around and between the tables, sent balls crashing from cushion to cushion, entered the boss's domain and drew himself a cup of tea and poured it down the sink, leaned on the counter to look around with a lordly air. Remembering the forbidden, the fact that no one was allowed to rest his body on a table to take a far-placed shot, he went to table one, climbed onto the green, lay on his back in the center and drummed his heels on the slate bed. He was delighted.

Paintwork in good shape, windows sparkling and drapes crisp-clean, the clapboard house stood out from its frowsy neighbors like a dime in a sweep's ear.

Being the kind of home Mrs. Chaps would be expected to have, Mr. Mortimer picked it out as he entered the street. Drawing closer, seeing the number, he smiled at the reliability of his cleaning woman.

He left his bicycle parked neatly at the gate. Using his little finger so as not to mar the immaculate surface of the brass, he rattled the knocker. The door opened.

Mrs. Chaps wore a flowered coverall, a scarf secured with a cameo, and her hair, glinting like polished steel, drawn back with particular smoothness into its bun. Was she also wearing make-up? No, that color was a blush.

"Good afternoon, Mr. Mortimer."

"Good afternoon, Mrs. Chaps."

"The rain's keeping off."

"Yes, it is."

"Won't you come in?"

"Thank you."

Mrs. Chaps led the way straight through into a back room, which bypassing of the parlor afforded Mr. Mortimer more than a little satisfaction. Being received in a ceremonious parlor crowned a guest with honor, yes, but not personal interest. The kitchen-lounge was for family and friends.

"Ah," Mr. Mortimer said, looking around the friendly room with appreciation. "You've got a cozy place here, Mrs. Chaps."

"Well, I must say, the new apartments isn't like these old houses."

"I couldn't agree more."

"These old ones make a real home."

"That's the word—home."

After Mr. Mortimer had made suitable comments about the photograph of a son in the merchant navy, he sat as directed at the table. To the plates of food Mrs. Chaps added an ancient Wedgwood teapot, on which she fitted a cozy, before sitting herself. "Well now," she said. "Dig in."

For the next fifteen minutes they were busy cutting bread, spreading jelly, slicing cake, speaking only to ask that the various doings be passed.

With a whimper of plump contentment, Mr. Mortimer

leaned back to taper off the meal with his third cup of tea and a final cookie. "Excellent," he murmured.

"So glad."

"Best feed I've had in a long while."

"I dare say it's nice to have a change from sandwiches at the hall."

"A most agreeable change."

"But I hope this hasn't interfered with your work."

"Not at all. I left a lad I know in charge."

"Good," said Mrs. Chaps. "Business is business, after all."

Admirable woman, thought Mr. Mortimer. Admirable. Business is business. Admirable. Which reminded him.

"Mrs. Chaps," he said, "I understand that all Marlake's cleaners are now getting a higher rate. Is that right?"

She looked embarrassed, like someone accused of being nice. "Well, I believe so."

Mr. Mortimer gave a firm nod. "In that case, starting tomorrow you will receive the new rate from me as well."

When Mrs. Chaps had finished mumbling her thanks she rose, and fetched a screw of newsprint, which she unwound to reveal a cigar. She handed it to her guest, saying, "It's a cigar."

Mr. Mortimer reddened with pleasure. "Thank you, Mrs. Chaps."

"A man should finish a meal with a good smoke, I always say."

"You know," Mr. Mortimer said, lighting up, "I don't believe I've had a cigar in thirty years." He puffed importantly. "Yes, thirty years. Not since the day I was married."

"Twenty-two years in April it'll be for me."

They spoke of weddings, of last-minute panics, drunken guests, arguing relatives, nausea; they spoke of honeymoons, of embarrassment and boredom; they spoke of marriage, of comfortableness and companionship.

"I'm surprised you never married again, Mrs. Chaps."

"I'm surprised too, that you didn't, Mr. Mortimer."

They looked out of the window. Their voices dropped.

Mr. Mortimer said, "I never really thought about it."

"Nor did I. It's a big step."

"A step in the dark unless you're sure."

"Unless you know someone real well."

"Known them for years, in fact."

"Seen them every day."

"Have the same outlook on life, business and so on."

"Like the same sort of things."

"Homey things."

"Yes," Mrs. Chaps said.

"Yes," Mr. Mortimer said.

There fell a solemn three-minute silence, during which hostess and guest drifted metaphorically away from each other to some misty cenotaph, there to reflect a while, remember, and perhaps, lay a wreath of good-bye.

The Great Erik sped in his Pontiac over the bridge which arcs gracefully between Windsor and Detroit. There had been no trouble on the Canadian side, he expected none on the American. And why should there be? A hundred thousand people a day crossed over the line. He had crossed several hundred times himself. There were no records kept.

As he stopped behind the line of cars waiting to pass through Immigration, Erik assured himself again that all this was not foolishly unnecessary, caution carried to idiot lengths. Yes, he could have gone to a store in Hamilton or Windsor, but there was just that tiny chance that he would be remembered afterward. It was the little things you had to watch, they had ruined many a brilliant scheme. Detroit was in another country, another world.

"How long you plan on staying, sir?" An Immigration officer peered in at him.

"Just for the evening. Going to take in a show."

"Identification?"

Erik showed his driver's license. The officer gave it a glance: "Okay." Erik drove on, slowing at the Customs building, speeding up again when a uniformed man waved him by.

82

Ten minutes later he parked on the Sears' lot and entered the store. In the crowded clothing department he walked along beside the racks of women's coats. Style was unimportant, so was material. What he wanted was the right color. He found it with ease. A bright red. The coats were lightweight gabardine, which, he thought approvingly, would bundle up small.

Selecting the correct size he took it to a salesgirl. He noted that he was not the only lone male shopper in the department. Nor did the girl appear to find anything odd in his purchasing a woman's coat.

Transaction over, he went off with his gaudy bag, telling himself to later buy a plain paper bag with a stiff top and string handles. With the coat draped carelessly over the car seat he would have no trouble with Canadian Customs. The odd purchase was, in any case, not the sort of thing they were concerned about.

Heading for another department it occurred to Erik how curious all this was, the strange way he was feeling, being in the States, making elaborate plans, his hopes set on murder. Everything had an air of fantasy. He wondered vaguely if he were dreaming.

At a cosmetic counter he bought an aerosol can of foam hand cream, and his shopping was over. As soon as he got back across the line he would telephone the poolroom—could be there were records kept of intercountry calls. He would ask for a conference. Or rather, he would *order* one. He was the top man of this little show.

Table number one, beside the counter, was being played on by the evening's first customers, three youths with the sparkle of recent scrubbings. They had an audience of a younger boy, who laughed at their every inane joke, tried to keep from gagging on his cigarette and pretended not to notice that he was being ignored.

Table five was also in use. When the Great Erik had telephoned an hour earlier to arrange a meeting, Mr. Mortimer had sent Lefty Steel to fetch the con man and had then put them to acting as if their presence were perfectly innocent. Because Oliver Jet was taking no interest in the game, was staring into space, Lefty played shot after shot and even moved balls into easier positions.

Lefty felt on top of the world. Everything was great. He only hoped that Erik wouldn't arrive too soon, that there would be time for other people apart from the three youths, who were being obvious about not looking, to come in and see him playing a game with no less a person than Oliver Jet.

Oliver's thoughts were with the illusionist. Was Erik serious or showing off? Would he turn up and say the caper had best be forgotten? Was he a phony?

Oliver sighed. He knew that more important than the answers to these questions was how he wanted them answered. Did he really want Erik to be genuine?

Mr. Mortimer stood at his post, drumming fingers. He was nervous about the robbery, the fixing of Dave Morgan, the fact that customers were arriving and would see the conferees, and that said customers would not be able to use table five.

One of the nearby youths began to whistle *Lili of Laguna*.

Like Satan before a crucifix, Mr. Mortimer's nervousness gave way before the force of pleasanter thoughts. The tea with Mrs. Chaps, he mused, had gone very well. They had reached, you might say, an understanding. At least, when he had said, jokingly, "Who'd have an old fogy like me?" she had said unjokingly, "Well, you know what they say, Mr. Mortimer: always follow a man with a dream." So there you are.

The swing doors twanged open and Satan stuck a black fingernail through Mr. Mortimer's chest to scratch his heart. Oliver Jet stiffened, his hands clamping tight around the cue he had been negligently holding. Lefty Steel raised himself slowly from a shooting stance.

The Great Erik had arrived.

He stood by the doors, pausing to collect himself. He had driven quickly, at times wildly. It was almost as if he had been trying to leave behind the ache in his stomach.

His ache receded as he walked to table five—finally he had beaten the confidence man at being the last in.

Lefty and Oliver stayed as they were and said nothing. Mr. Mortimer came bustling down the hall and hissed, "Hadn't we best go out on the landing?"

His pleasure increased by being indubitably the man of the moment, Erik sat on a chair and said a lazy, "No."

"Er, does that mean . .   ?"

"It means that going outside would be too obvious. No one can hear what we're saying"

Mr. Mortimer looked behind, cringed and nodded.

Still lazy, Erik said, "Everything at my end is under control."

Lefty: "You mean we pull the job?"

"Yes."

The three men gave sighs, like babies full of milk and queasiness.

Oliver patted a bulky pocket. "I've got the gun."

"I'll get my uncle's car," Lefty said.

Erik tipped a brief nod to acknowledge the others' words. "After giving this some thought," he said, "I've decided the best time is just before I go onstage. It will be dark. Better for Mrs. Vandle's, better for Morgan. Agreed?"

The other men nodded.

"I have also decided that, since time is of the essence, we will do the job tonight."

Lefty grinned, Mr. Mortimer's cheeks trembled and Oliver had a shrinking sensation inside him.

"Agreed?" asked Erik, and when the other men had again nodded said, "Let's get the details straight."

FOUR

Lefty Steel had treated himself to a bath, the first since July. Now he was dressing. He put on a pink shirt and a tie featuring a naked woman, new blue slacks and white-on-black shoes.

From its hiding place he brought out and strapped on his gun. The effect was beautiful, he thought, posing in front of the mirror. He kept on looking while slipping into his best jacket, a lapel-less garment in thick cloth of a dark maroon.

Another minute he spent in admiration, watching himself light a cigarette, whipping out and casually replacing his gun, before heading for the kitchen.

His father looked round from the sink. "All dolled up, eh?"

"Yeah."

"Heavy date?"

"Not specially."

"Why not come to the Waterloo for a beer with your old man?"

Lefty shook his head. He asked, as he had asked many times, "Why d'you drink so much?"

"Well, you know . . . now your mother's not here . . . a bit lonely . . ."

It was the usual excuse and one which Lefty knew to be untrue. In life his mother had also been overfond of alcohol. His earliest recollection was of sitting in a baby carriage outside a bar, numb with cold and clutching an icy bottle of milk in which floated congealed lumps of fat. As far back as unbroken memory went, both parents had spent all their free time out drinking. He had found nothing in them worthy of respect.

"There'll be the fights on television," his father said persuasively. "See some real action."

Lefty shrugged and walked out.

In the dark street he set off to walk to his uncle's house and borrow the car that would be standing outside; by borrow meaning he would get into the car and use the keys which were always left in the ashtray.

Walking, he began to think about the caper. But there was nothing to think about. He thought about something else.

A lamp with a feeble bulb lit dimly a bedroom above the doughnut shop. On the bed lay Oliver Jet, hands clasped on his stomach, eyes wandering along ceiling cracks. Pel was sitting on a chair. The room was quiet.

Pel wondered if Oliver was sick. For close on an hour now, since coming home and announcing bluntly to her and Jonesy that tonight was the night for the swindle, he had lain on the bed and stared at the ceiling without saying a word. He had been moody lately, but never like this. If he wasn't sick, he must be worried about the job. Or scared.

She stretched out her hand. "Ollie?"

He sat up, took the hand and held it tightly. "It's time I went."

"Feeling all right?"

He nodded. "Pel?"

"Yes, Ollie?"

"You won't ever leave me, will you?"

"No," she said, and squeezed his hand. "I won't never leave you."

The poolhall was crowded and noisy, every table occupied, watchers and waiters thick around the sides.

As he served snacks, reckoned charges, added names to the waiting list and made change, doing nothing with his usual perfection, Mr. Mortimer threw glances constantly at the clock and at the wall telephone. A dew of sweat glistened on his brow. Every time the doors twanged, his heart twanged. Every time someone shouted, he twitched. Every time he was addressed he said, "What?"

In order to keep himself from worrying about the robbery proper, his worry was given to one of its peripheral players, the telephone. Whenever anyone veered close to it he would stop what he was doing, and stare; and stare until the danger was past.

The telephone would be needed soon. What if someone began to make a call and refused to ring off?

His heated blood oozed onto his brow sweat enough to gather in drops, which ran like slow tears of despair down either side of his nose.

Finally, the crowd thickening so much that the telephone was in danger of being hidden, he could stand the strain no longer. *Out of Order* he scrawled on a card, which he took across and propped behind the receiver.

Back in his place, he started to dwell on the robbery's other, more frightening aspects. His twitching and heart-twanging and sweating increased. He threw the telephone a wistful glance.

It was intermission time at the Grand. Erik was in the stalls refreshment bar, crowded with people from the audience. Wearing full stage regalia, Erik was sipping a Coke and letting himself be stared at.

He felt uplifted, filled by a sense of well being. It was like that curious and pleasant feeling that comes to a host when, dressed and polished and with everything ready, he waits for his first guest to arrive. This pause in time was a favorite of Erik's. His most popular daydreams used to be those in which, after some heady success, he was slowly approaching Miranda—forever approaching—and with loving Miranda waiting—forever waiting.

There had been a recent shower, which, along Lakeshore Drive, had dampened no spirits nor stopped any action. Heads and hats glistened with water, feet splashed through puddles. The crowd streamed thickly, forming into crests around the more successful amusements. The area was brighter than tropic noon from the flashing lights and there was a manic blare of noise.

Oliver Jet stood at the corner of Waterloo Street. He stood in a sag. Never had he felt so alien to the mass. The scene almost frightened him; it seemed about to reach a crescendo and burst. Instinctively he moved back to the wall, when, realizing his action, he told himself to sharpen up and look alive. Which telling, apart from a bodily re-action, had no effect. The inner man continued to quail. He was afraid. Of everything. He would have been afraid if the streets were deserted. He was ready to give in, re-treat. He wanted to change his mind.

And he could, he thought suddenly. It was not too late. He could tell the others he was out. If they insisted on going through with it themselves he would create an alibi. He could pretend to be drunk and get safely arrested.

And he would. He'd do it.

Oliver's throat tightened with the emotion of release.

A car stopped at the curb. Inside sat Lefty Steel. He was dressed as if going to a party, dressed in a way that would make him howlingly memorable to the least retentive mind. He was ridiculous. The whole scheme was ridiculous.

Oliver felt a sad bubble of a laugh working up against the relief in his throat. How could he have ever let himself get as far as this? Ridiculous!

Lefty Steel leaned over, opened the passenger door, pushed it wide and jerked his head.

Pel made Oliver cross to the car, get in, close the door and say, "Let's go."

The Great Erik sat in his dressing room looking at the second hand of his watch. When the hand reached what he considered the desired point, he stood up, lifted the aerosol can, left the dressing room and knocked on the door next to his.

"Yes?"

"Erik."

"Come in, darling."

Erik closed his eyes briefly in hatred before opening the door.

Miranda sat at her mirror, dressed for the stage. She was peering closely at her eyelashes. "I'll be on in a moment."

"I just brought you this thing I got today," Erik said, looking aside at the clothes hung on a row of pegs. Among other garments were two coats, one green, one bright red.

Miranda turned. "A present?"

"If you can call it that. It cost less than a dollar."

"How sweet, darling. What is it?"

"Hand cream. See, you press this—"

From the can shot a spray of white. While Miranda gasped with alarm, Erik, pretending the release knob was stuck down, pretending hissed annoyance, liberally sprayed the green topcoat.

He let the knob up. "Damn," he said, then, "My God, look what I've done to your coat."

"Oh dear."

Erik put on an act of embarrassed apology, stammering and rubbing his brow. His distress was such that Miranda was forced into the part of consoler. She patted him, laughed, told him not to worry.

"When it dries it won't be seen. And it was so sweet of you, buying me this."

"But . . ."

Miranda turned her head at the sound of music. "I'm on. My great moment has arrived, tra-la." She swept out with, "See you, darling."

Erik waited a moment and then spat on the mirror.

Jonesy looked up quickly from his newspaper as Pel came into the room. She was frowning in puzzlement. "Funny," she said.

"What?" asked Jonesy. "Something wrong?"

"Well, I was going to wash out my stockings, like I do every night, and I can't find them. They've gone. Disappeared."

Jonesy shrugged. He was returning to the newspaper

when Pel went on, "And before Ollie left I saw him put something in his pocket at the dresser. He must have taken them!"

Jonesy stared. "Ollie took your stockings?"

Pel giggled. "What on earth would he do that for?"

"Ollie took your stockings?"

Pel's attitude changed as she saw the look on Jonesy's face. "What's wrong? Does it mean something?"

Jonesy dropped his paper. He got up slowly, tautly. "Yes, it means something," he said as if to himself, nodding. "There's only one thing it can mean. He's gone to do a job. Not a con, a job. Robbery."

"Robbery? Ollie?"

"Right. And for that he needs your stockings."

"The stockings are for masks!" Pel cried, pointing at Jonesy.

"Right again. He must've got in with some hood." Jonesy ran a quick hand through his hair. "Well well well."

Looking at Jonesy's flushed face and bright eyes, Pel asked, "Good?"

"Good? I'll say it's good." He began to pace. "This means cash money, not a check. Cash." He stopped in front of Pel. "Which means we don't need to wait. We could pull out at once. So now it's up to you. You've got to make up your mind."

"I've made it up," she said coldly. She swung around and walked into the bedroom.

Erik pushed through the swing doors into the poolhall. He wore a coat over his stage clothes. The hall was crowded and smoky. No one paid any attention to the man in the penumbra who went to the telephone. Erik blinked at a sign saying *Out of Order*.

"I put it there," hissed Mr. Mortimer, appearing jerkily beside him and pulling off the sign. Erik fed the coin slot and dialed. He felt superiorly calm compared to the other.

"The Vandle residence," said a female voice.

Not attempting to disguise his tone, merely speeding up

his speech, Erik cuddled the receiver close and said, "I'd like to speak to Mr. Morgan, please."

"He's in his room. Shall I go get him?"

"That's the idea, yes. Tell him John Constance of *Spotlight* has to talk to him at once."

"Okay. John Whosit?"

"Constance."

"John Constance of what did you say?"

"*Spotlight*," snapped Erik. "It's a theatrical weekly."

"Oh yes. There's some in the house. Real interesting. And you're with *Spotlight*?"

"Miss," said Erik testily, "would you please bring Mr. Morgan to the telephone."

"Well, okay. I was only asking. Excuse *me*. I'll get him now. Hold on."

Erik shook his head at Mr. Mortimer, who made an attempt at a sympathetic smile as he threw worried looks at those standing close.

The line came alive: "Dave Morgan speaking."

"Hello there," Erik said. "This is Constance of *Spotlight*."

"How do you do." Morgan sounded suitably impressed.

"I haven't much time so I'll get right to business. I'm planning a series on artistes who use no words or songs in their acts and I'd appreciate it if we could meet now for a brief chat."

"I see, I see."

"Unfortunately I can spare only ten minutes, starting a quarter of an hour from now. My schedule is most rigid. I'm at Johnny Rock's dressing room and I'm meeting Angela Smirke just after seeing you."

"Couldn't we meet later?"

"Afraid not. Immediately after seeing Miss Smirke I'm getting a train back to Toronto."

"In that case, Mr. Constance, of course I'll meet you."

"Fine. How about making the place that building in the center of the park?"

"Oh, very well."

"Rather an odd place to meet, I know, but it happens to be midway between my other appointments."

"Okay, Mr. Constance, in fifteen minutes at the park center."

"See you soon." Swiftly, Erik depressed the cradle, released it again, shot coins into the slot and dialed. The double ring of a call signal sounded. He smiled with relief, handed the receiver to Mr. Mortimer and walked to the doors.

"Marlake eight-five-one-seven-five."

"Oh, er, hello," said Mr. Mortimer hoarsely, shoulders hunched, lips touching the mouthpiece and cupped by his hand. "Is that Miss Farmer?"

"I beg your pardon?" said the ex-matron. "I can't hear you."

He raised his voice. "Is that Miss Farmer?"

"Yes."

Slow, he cautioned himself; drag it out. "The same Miss Farmer that used to be at High View Hospital?"

"Yes, I was matron there. Who is this, please?"

"Well, I don't suppose you recognize my voice, do you?"

"I'm afraid I do not," she said. "What's the name, please?"

"I, er, wonder if you'll remember it."

"Let's see, shall we?"

A burst of laughter came from one of the tables. Mr. Mortimer shuddered, clasped his sweaty hands tighter on the instrument and said, "Sorry about the noise, Miss Farmer. I'm calling from a cafe."

"And the name?"

"As a matter of fact it's William Brown. B . . . r . . . o . . . w . . . n."

"I don't believe I know a William Brown."

"Oh dear. I was hoping you'd remember."

Silence from the other end. Mr. Mortimer gasped, "Hello, hello?"

"I'm still here," she said quietly. "And I'm wondering."

"Oh?"

"Yes, I'm wondering if Mr. Brown is the man who'd lost himself yesterday and wanted to know the time."

"I don't understand."

"Then we're both in the same boat. Good night—"

"Wait, wait. Listen, please. I was a patient in High View. Seven years ago. Don't you remember me? William Brown?"

"Well . . ."

"Oh, I know you must have had hundreds of patients through your hands. And I know everyone wanted your attention because you were the most popular matron in the place. But I felt sure you'd recall me. We were quite friendly. I'm disappointed."

"Well, I'm sorry."

"I remember you perfectly, Miss Farmer. You always had a kind word for everybody, and you were especially nice to me. It was the highlight of my day when you made your rounds."

Miss Farmer's voice had lost its chill. "Perhaps it will come to me in a minute, Mr. Brown. What were you in for?"

Erik was smiling to himself as he strode down the alley beside the theater. All arranged as neat as could be. Dave Morgan would be waiting, drawn by the only thing he couldn't resist: the smell of greasepaint. Whatever other plans he might have, he couldn't resist that.

"He's a long time," said Lefty Steel.

Oliver Jet grunted.

They were sitting in the car, which was parked in the trees facing the Vandle house. Lefty was keyed-up, eager for action, making him more talkative than normal. He had tried several times to start a conversation. Result: nothing. His companion sat as silent and still as a zombie.

Just like a lousy zombie, Lefty thought. He tried again. "What d'you reckon Morgan's doing?"

No answer. Lefty supplied it himself. "Trying to phone that nurse woman, I guess. What if he gets through? What if old Mortimer can't keep her on the line, or what if Morgan got to her first?"

"Ah well," he went on, "it doesn't make much difference. We can handle the nurse too, if she comes. What's another woman more or less? We could even take on a few guys if we had to."

Nothing from Oliver Jet.

Lefty was about to snort with annoyance when the reason for Oliver's attitude came to him. Instead of snorting he blushed. Oliver Jet was a pro, and this was the way pros were on a job: silent, smooth, tough. Not chattering like kids.

Lefty could have kicked himself. He sank down in the seat. Resisting the urge to make some sort of amends he closed his mouth tight, bulging the lips smoothly and toughly.

The dressing-room telephone rang. Miranda looked at the instrument in surprise. It was rare she got a call here. Shrugging, putting down her jar of face cream, she rose and lifted the receiver.

"Hello," said a gruff voice. "This is Dave. Dave Morgan."

Miranda was even more surprised. "Dave Morgan?"

"Right. Now get this and get it straight. I'm in a hurry."

"What is all this?"

"Just listen, baby. Listen good. I'm in trouble. I need fifty bucks, fast, like now."

"So?"

"So you're going to give it me."

Miranda laughed. "You're out of your strong-man mind."

"Am I?"

"You sure are."

"Get this, baby. I'm in bad trouble, fuzz trouble. Right now I don't give one goddamn about anything or anyone. I'm mean, I don't care who I hurt if I don't get that fifty bucks. You'd better bring it right away."

"And if I don't?"

"Then I'll just have to tell Erik about you and me."

Miranda stared at the wall. She listened dazedly while

95

the voice told her where to go and repeated what would happen if she wasn't there in five minutes.

"Hold on here," she said weakly.

"That's all, baby. Five minutes."

Oliver Jet said, "Here he comes."

Shooting up from his slouch Lefty saw Dave Morgan close off the house doorway's oblong of light and stride to the garage.

"Run down to the corner," Oliver Jet said. "If he turns left at the end of the next street, that means he's going to the matron's."

"If he don't, he still could've called her."

"No. She'd have been here by now."

"Maybe."

"Get going, before he drives out."

Not sure that he liked being ordered around, particularly as he was packing a rod, Lefty got out of the car and went at a fast clip down the street. He and the Cadillac reached the corner together.

Dave Morgan braked hesitantly at the junction. Miss Farmer's number had been engaged: Should he go round to her house?

Morgan decided not. There was not enough time. The Constance man wouldn't wait. There was nothing to worry about in any case. Everything would be okay at the house, he would be back soon, Ellie had promised to keep the outing quiet, Mrs. Vandle would never know he'd been away. And the *Spotlight* thing was too good to miss. An article about his eager plans for more theater work might ease suspicion, suggest he had been done away with by the person unknown who was really responsible for the robbery, and if not, the photograph he would give Constance, one taken when he was younger and thinner, could hardly be a drawback.

Morgan took his foot off the brake and sped on.

Tomorrow night, he thought, it would be good-bye to

Marlake. This morning the old bird had checked her safe, with the usual frills and nonsense.

Morgan congratulated himself on how well he had done. What had looked like a nothing job had developed into a bonanza. He had played the whole thing as cool as ice. He had made no close friends in town and had brushed off any past acquaintances he had come across. There was, of course, that little blonde piece from the chorus at the Grand, but she was just screw material, a guy shouldn't starve himself, and he hadn't gotten too involved. There was no room in the pie for a second finger, male or female. Yes, he had played it smart. He was no fool.

Morgan smiled at the memory of the Great Erik. That had been an enjoyable two minutes, spanking the short-ass. Great. And calling him a cuckold, that really got him where the cheese turns green. Everyone knew that Erik was jealous of his own shadow, a spoiled overage brat whose only friends in show biz were the bottom-rungers who would never be anything else.

Morgan wondered if Erik knew that the man he had seen him with one day, Oliver Jet, was a confidence trickster. He hoped not. And he hoped Jet would take the brat for every dime he owned.

Humming, Dave Morgan sped on toward the park.

"It's okay," Lefty Steel said, looking in the window of the car. "No nurse."

"Get in," Oliver Jet said.

"What for?"

"We'll give it another five minutes."

"Why?"

"Let Morgan get to where he's going, that's why."

"He won't be back."

"Still, the matron might show up."

"You just said she would've been here by now."

"Best to make sure."

Because Oliver Jet was a pro, Lefty got in the car. He slumped in his seat, silent and smooth and tough.

Erik, backstage at the Grand, had moved away from the telephone after calling Miranda and pretending to be Dave Morgan. Now he stood in the wings, working hard at not showing his agitation while ostensibly watching the Irish tenor run through his act. In fifteen minutes he was due onstage himself. Why the hell didn't she come down?

But if she didn't go to meet Morgan, he thought hopefully, that would mean she was innocent.

Nervously, Erik mouthed an intro-joke with the singer onstage. Now there was fourteen minutes left.

He heard a door being closed, heard descending steps on the iron staircase. He turned. Miranda reached ground level and came toward him. She looked as normal after a performance. Perhaps she was going home, he thought, while noting that she wore the red topcoat, and slacks—had she put them on over her costume?

"Hello, Erik darling."

He forced himself to smile. "Going out?"

"Home. I've got a headache."

"Sorry, honey. Get something for it."

"I will. And there's other things I need while I'm at the drugstore. Big things. Cosmetics."

"Yes?"

"I've no money with me. I never have, as you know. Could you loan me fifty dollars?"

"I'm sorry," said Miss Farmer, "I can't hear you again. You'll have to speak louder."

Mr. Mortimer pressed a hand to his brow, which rang with pain. He thought that if he had to keep this William Brown thing up a moment longer he would drop foaming at the mouth. He said:

"And there was the time you talked about your house."

"Wait a minute. You still haven't answered my question. Why did they keep you in for three months with a septic finger?"

"Did I say three months?"

"Yes."

"I meant two."

"Two months then. Why so long with only a septic finger?"

"Er, complications."

"What kind?"

"It—"

"Mr. Mortimer," shouted a voice in his ear. "We'd like three Cokes, please."

"What was that?" asked Miss Farmer.

"What?" said Mr. Mortimer dazedly.

The matron repeated her question while the customer repeated his order. Mr. Mortimer gave in. He was dizzy and trembling and steeped in sweat, his head was cracking. Surely, he thought, looking at the wall clock, surely Miss Farmer had been kept on the line long enough.

He said, "I've got to go. Emergency. I'll call you later." Flopping the receiver into its cradle he walked unsteadily to the counter, circled it and sank into his chair.

A head appeared above. "We'd like three—"

"In a minute!" yelled Mr. Mortimer, his voice high. "In a minute!"

The two stage hands, the juggler from the first half of the show and the pair of chorus girls took no notice as the Great Erik strolled into dimness. His stroll, once he was fully out of sight, changed to an urgent striding. He sped down the concrete ramp to the stage-doorkeeper cubbyhole.

Into the recess he put his top hat. He brought out his raincoat, which had been left there after calling Morgan from the poolroom. He put the coat on, holding himself back from slipshod haste: even though he had only eleven minutes left a few extra seconds could make no difference.

He took off and put away his eye patch, brought from the recess the carrier bag which held the red coat, a last pat of his pockets while mentally naming their contents: gun, scarf, cotton. He was ready.

Slipping outside he walked to the street. No passer-by gave him a glance as he headed away from Lakeshore Drive. He crossed the railroad line and turned onto a quiet street.

There was no one about. He began to run, clutching the bag with both arms.

He slowed back to a stride on reaching the large block whose far side faced the park, went into the alley and stopped. Although dim as expected, he could see the junction of the alleys clearly. And Miranda was not there.

He felt a surge of alarm. Miranda should have been there waiting, to meet Dave Morgan, or so she thought.

Erik ran lightfooted along the alley. As he reached the junction he saw, beyond it, at the alley's entry into the park square, one of the passers-by stop and peer inward. He leaped for the wall. The one who had stopped was Miranda.

What the hell is she doing out there? he seethed.

Miranda turned around, lifted her head suddenly and walked off toward the park.

The area alongside the golf course was heavily silent, lightly lit, the picture of peace. Yet there was no peace in the heart and mind of Lefty Steel. He was swollen to bursting point with impatience. Oliver Jet, he thought, was carrying the smooth bit too far. He was sitting on and on and on.

Twisting round from the steering wheel Lefty blurted, "It's time to go, eh?"

Oliver gave a start. He had almost got himself convinced that nothing was happening, that he was merely sitting in a car to pass time, that soon they would drive on and have a drink somewhere. Lefty's outburst was like a drenching with cold water. Oliver rubbed his upper arms.

"Well?" the younger man asked, eyebrows jigging. "Is it time or not?"

"Yes, it's time."

"Come on then, let's go let's go."

"All right."

Miranda had been surprised to see Dave Morgan waiting in the park center and not, as he had said on the phone, down the service alley, where she herself had waited until nervousness of the gloom had sent her out, assuming that the ex-wrestler would find her if she stayed close.

Now she was walking toward the park. Her surprise had gone. Her feelings had returned to where they had been since the telephone call: a misery of anger, frustration, and misgiving.

Dave Morgan, she thought, this man whom she hardly knew, had turned into the lowest bastard imaginable. Blackmailing the guilty was disgusting enough, blackmailing the innocent was surely twice as rotten. But Morgan was shrewd, to give the slob his due. Familiar with Erik's jealous nature, he knew that he would be inclined to fall for the Iago bit, and knew that she knew it too. How could she possibly prove to Erik that she had gone no further with Morgan than a handshake? The story could ruin everything between them, which would be tragic, for her love for Erik was strong and true, despite his jealousies, his pettiness, and the fact that basically he was weak. She loved him.

Miranda turned into the park.

Lefty Steel leaped from the car, Oliver Jet got out slowly. Lefty marched across the road, Oliver followed at a walk. Lefty ran to the gateway, Oliver went almost on tiptoe. Lefty stepped openly into the drive, Oliver moved close to the hedge. Lefty strode, making gestures for haste, Oliver continued as before.

Two windows of the house had light-brightened curtains; one above, one below, both at the rear end of the side. There was no sound from within.

Reaching the door, panting, Lefty raised his fist to knock.

Oliver hurried, brought out of himself by the other's stupidity, and hurrying hissed, "Stop that!"

Lefty dropped his arm, danced his shoulders. "What's wrong now?"

Oliver reached him. "Keep your voice down, you fool."

"What for?" Lefty asked, lowering his volume a fraction.

"They'll hear us. They might call the cops."

"Okay. But why shouldn't I knock? That's what we're gonna do, ain't it?"

"Not until we're masked."

Again the younger man felt like kicking himself. "Oh," he said, "yes." While watching Oliver Jet bring out and untangle two nylon stockings, he added, "I wasn't gonna knock really."

They pulled the stockings over their heads, tucking the dangling legs into their shirt collars. Looking at each other, they were shocked. Their faces had become unrecognizable masses of squashed brown flesh. They could have been burn victims, or extras in a movie about the march of science.

With Oliver, his stocking served fully the psychological function of the mask: he felt safer, vaguely immune, protected. Lefty Steel felt foolish. His mind rejected the stocking as destructive to his appearance. Besides, real gangsters never wore such things.

"Ready?" Oliver asked.

"Sure."

"All right. Knock."

Erik, near the alley's mouth, stared at Miranda. She was drawing close to Dave Morgan in the center of Marlake Park.

Erik realized what must have happened. He further realized that his plan was not necessarily spoiled. While there would be no point in wearing the coat and scarf to shoot Morgan and then lead possible chasers into the alley, where Miranda would have been found, he could still use the disguise and still shoot Dave Morgan.

In fact, Erik thought with a grin, Miranda being right there made the whole thing perfect. It was better than the original.

With all haste Erik retreated into deeper gloom and began to change. He didn't have the nerve to look at his watch to see how much time he had left.

He took off his raincoat and stuffed it into the bag, after pulling out the coat of bright red. This he put on and buttoned. From its pocket he brought a scarf, which he put over his head and tied peasant-style under his chin. He decided against tucking the wad of cotton under the scarf front to simulate blond hair; the coat, the headgear, the heavy cosmetics on his face—these were enough.

Leaving the bag on the step of a doorway he set off at a fast walk. He was trembling.

Across the street, through a gateway and onto a gravel path he went. Near the public lavatory Morgan and Miranda stood facing each other, separated by two yards. The strong man was leaning forward, wearing a puzzled expression. Miranda was talking.

Speeding up his pace, as his heart had speeded up, Erik took a side path, circled round to be to the rear of Miranda and stopped in a spinney of saplings thirty feet from where the couple stood.

Dave Morgan, still looking puzzled, was shaking his head. There was no one else around.

Erik got out the gun. Using both hands he lifted it at arms' length and aimed for the center of Morgan's chest.

Erik was frightened: by what he was doing and by the sick speed of his heart and by the fact that the gun kept veering to the side.

He forced his arms to a trembling stiffness, held his breath and pulled the trigger.

He stepped back from the recoil and the noise, he jerked forward again with a grunted cry at what he saw.

The back of Miranda's head had exploded into a crimson star. She crashed to the ground.

At last, in answer to the third knock, there came the sound of footsteps from inside the house of Mrs. Vandle.

Oliver Jet tensed, Lefty Steel stuck forward his chin.

The door opened to flush the men with light. The maid was a dumpy woman of thirty with a plain face and her hair covered with a net. She got as far as, "Yes, what . . . ?" before at last seeing the visitors, by which time they were moving inside and her gasping grab for the door was too late.

They crowded her back against the wall, their hands poised for restraining. But the maid was malleable with shock. She drooped on the wall like a hung coat, eyes stupid, disbelieving, as they stared at the masks.

"The door," Oliver hissed.

Lefty marched to the door and swung it closed. Turning, he remembered his gun. He pulled it out with an elaborately nonchalant movement of shoulder and arm as he returned to the others.

Seeing the gun, Oliver jerked, "What the—" He broke off, ducking his head at the noise.

The maid's eyes grew more stupid yet as they found the revolver. Oliver, thinking the woman might scream, grabbed her arm and said, "Into the kitchen."

"What was that?"

"Come on, only a car."

"I didn't hear nothing."

"Firecracker, hon."

The voices floated over from the sidewalks to the center of Marlake Park.

Miranda lay on the gravel, no movement in her body. Dave Morgan, slowly rising from a brief examination, stared at the blood on his hand.

Erik was retreating step by step. He was amazed, shattered, petrified. He was hardly aware of his actions. He knew that Miranda was dead, she had to be, and he was the one who had killed her. It was fantastic.

"I didn't do it," he muttered abruptly, in a deep gruffness at the back of his throat. "I didn't mean it."

More voices, louder now:

"Sounded like a gun."

"Oh, for Chrissakes."

"It was over this way."

Erik became conscious of the gun he held down at his side. He found enough reason to give himself orders. He stopped moving and feverishly worked the automatic into his pocket.

When he looked up again he saw that he was being stared at by Dave Morgan.

His face wearing a small smile of amazement, the ex-wrestler slowly began to raise a hand, of which the index finger was pointed.

Erik found more reason. He turned away and started to walk. Jerky at first, his walk became firmer as his speed increased.

Two men were striding toward him. They asked, "What was that?" and, "Was it a gun?"

Erik kept going, the men went on. He turned through a gateway and onto the road. On the sidewalk a couple stared at him curiously. He continued at the same pace. He was still turning over the fantastic notion that Miranda was dead and he responsible. All he had wanted was for her to be blamed for Morgan's murder. Now it might be the reverse.

Dodging between moving cars he reached the alley and went in. At the waiting carrier bag he stopped. There were no sounds of chase. He looked back. No one had followed.

Numbly he changed coats, took off the scarf. More reason came. He began to walk as he bundled up the red gabardine and shoved it in the bag. Looking at his watch he saw that in two minutes he was due onstage. Two minutes!

He drew a fast breath and shot forward into a run.

Mr. Mortimer moved on unsteady legs to the counter end, where, fingering his lips, he looked around the poolhall. With alarm he had just remembered that he had not yet done anything about the alibi for Lefty and Oliver. He must do it at once.

Creating the pseudo-alibi would be quite simple. All he had to do was visit one end of the room and drop some remark made by Oliver Jet, who, he would say, was at the other end, then do the same thing built around Lefty Steel in a different part of the hall.

According to the confidence man, this would ease into people's minds the firm belief that he and Lefty were present. It had to be done casually, however, not be obvious.

"Pack of Players, please," a customer said.

"Back in a bit," Mr. Mortimer murmured absently, stepping from his post.

"Feeling okay?" asked another man as he moved out of the way. "You look pale."

Mr. Mortimer said, "Back in a bit." He went through the standing audience to table five. The surrounding men were watching in silence a top player taking repeated shots of a run. Mr. Mortimer glanced up at the clock and cleared his throat.

In the large kitchen of Mrs. Vandle's house, the maid, who appeared dumbfounded rather than frightened, was sitting floppily in the armchair into which she had been pushed. One on either side of her stood Oliver Jet and Lefty Steel, faces sweating inside their stocking masks.

Now that the caper was actually under way, Oliver was feeling better, less nervous, more in control of himself, no longer in a state of dead desperation. The added fear brought by Lefty's gun had diminished; the gun, he had reasoned, was sure to be a harmless toy.

Again he asked of the maid, "Which is the old woman's room? Quick!"

Again she merely stared at him like an imbecile.

"I bet I can make her talk," Lefty growled.

"Shut up."

"We're wasting time."

"No violence."

"Anyway," said the younger man irritably, "what's it matter which room? Try 'em all."

"And she might hear? And she might lock the door?"

"We'll break it down."

"And she might have a phone extension and call the cops?"

"So we'll knock out the phone downstairs."

Oliver said lamely, "Oh."

Lefty stretched his mask with a smile: the pro wasn't *that* goddamn pro.

Oliver recovered some of the order in his voice. "You know how to do it?"

"Sure. Anyone does."

"Go and do it then."

Swinging round, Lefty strode from the kitchen and across the hallway to a telephone, which, after putting down his gun with care, he set about disabling.

Lefty was feeling peculiar. Not himself at all. Light and strange and different. He wasn't sure if the center of this odd sensation was in his body or his head; he wasn't even sure if the sensation was bad or good. All he knew was, he was not his usual self.

Had Lefty been capable of analysis and analogy he would have realized his feeling was in extended form akin to that of an actor when making an exit after having thrown his whole being into the character he was portraying: reality gives him pause: for a fleet moment he wonders, Who am I?

Erik burst through the stage door of the Grand. Gasping, he stood and listened. Applause. The end of the penultimate act. Erik was on.

Into the doorkeeper's cubbyhole he threw the carrier bag, took off and threw after it his raincoat, picked up his top hat and put it on.

From the stage, a fanfare of music, the prelude to his introduction.

Erik strolled up the concrete ramp and came backstage. Of the handful of people present, only one looked at him; looked and came across with, "You're on."

Erik, still out of breath, and knowing his face was a mass of nervous movements, bent down to brush at his knees. "I know."

Onstage, the MC said, "*And now the moment you've all been waiting for . . .*"

"Where's your eye patch?" the producer asked.

Straightening, Erik raised a protective hand to his face. "I—er—oh yes."

"Never knew you to forget that before."

While putting on his patch, making himself do it calmly, Erik searched for an excuse to explain his mistake. He gave the job up. He told himself it was far more important to give all his concentration to performing well.

"... *the Great Erik!*"

"Excuse me," Erik said. He walked to the wings, paused and walked to the footlights.

You are calm, he insisted. You are quite calm. You are going to concentrate hard on doing the act properly. You are not going to think about Miranda or anything connected with her.

Smiling unsteadily toward the audience he produced playing cards. The flick of his wrist which should have sent the pack into a sweeping fan sent it instead into a flutter across the footlights.

Marlake Park. By the center building there was a crowd, a growing crowd, people coming along the paths, some slowly with heads raised, others running. Present were two police constables. One was keeping the gawpers away from the body, the other was among the group which surrounded Dave Morgan.

Morgan was only now shaking himself free of the daze that had begun to form when Miranda had arrived with her incomprehensible talk of blackmail and had sprung to adulthood with the shot and her collapse. The past five minutes had been a turmoil of milling people, shouting voices and barked questions.

The questions were still going on. As before, he had no answers. He was thinking of the moments following the shot. That woman with the gun. He knew her face. He knew it well but couldn't place it, couldn't give it name or background.

Morgan started as his arm was shaken. He frowned at the constable, who said, "Come on, Mac, wake up."

A voice said, "Doped."

Another said, "Stoned."

"Shuttup," the uniformed man snarled. He sounded nervous. "Get the hell away."

No one moved. The constable seemed not to mind;

seemed glad even. He asked, "Again now, Mac, what's your name?"

"A woman," Morgan said.

"Yes yes," the constable said with hammy patience, "we know it's a woman. Tell me things I don't know. Your name, her name, and what you've done with the gun."

Involuntarily, Morgan reached out and gave the policeman a push. "Get away from me."

The surrounding group, drawing a breath of appreciation, stepped back. The constable, putting a hand on the butt of his revolver, stepped forward.

"Watch it, fella, watch it," he said.

Morgan began to turn. "Just get away from me."

"Don't move!"

Turning back, Morgan lashed out with his fist. He hit the constable and sent him staggering. A man leaped forward. Morgan met him with a short, hard right. The man dropped. Morgan swung away and ran.

When Mr. Mortimer, grown doubly nervous by the wait, had decided to interrupt the run on table five to speak his piece, the player interrupted himself by miscueing. He stood back, shaking his head.

Mr. Mortimer gave a sharp laugh. Every head jerked in his direction. The player asked, "What's so funny about that?"

"No, no," Mr. Mortimer said, tapping the player's shoulder. "I wasn't laughing at you. I was laughing at something Mr. Jet said just now." He looked around. "And we all know who Mr. Jet is, don't we? Ha-ha."

One or two men nodded. The player turned to watch his opponent take his shot.

"Yes," said Mr. Mortimer, "he's down the other end there. You can see him. Well, almost. He's behind those men. Oh, he's there all right. Oh yes."

His opponent having failed to make a point, the player made to move away, go around the table to the white. Mr. Mortimer grabbed his arm:

"Hold on. Wait a bit. Let me tell you what Mr. Jet said."

The player tutted. "This is an important game, Mr. Mortimer."

"Yes, yes. It'll only take a minute. Very funny. A scream. He said it just now. At the other end there. Mr. Jet. He's at the other end there."

"Well, come on, let's hear it."

"A scream."

"So all right—what?"

"Er," said Mr. Mortimer. He breathed heavily away his agitation. Sagging, he added an unhappy, "I've forgotten."

The upper hall of the Vandle house was long and broad, doors on each side and a window at the end. Silent, a single lamp gave the soft illumination.

With Lefty downstairs in charge of the still-speechless maid, Oliver Jet had stealthily tried one row of doors. They were unlocked and led into rooms without occupants.

Now, about to start on the other side, he thought of a short cut. Stooping low he looked at the sills. One, at the end, showed light.

He walked to the door and gently turned the handle. There was no lock. He stepped into a large room, halting on the threshold. His mouth felt dry, his heart made great pounds.

The room, lit by ornate table lamps, was furnished to choking with heavy Edwardian mammoths and minutes. Contrariwise, the bed was a simple cot. Against one wall stood a safe six feet high.

Head and body still, Oliver swept his gaze twice around the room before he saw, with a start, its occupant. She sat in a lamp's penumbra, watching quietly.

Mrs. Vandle was a bulky woman, strong looking, her shoulders broad under the dressing gown. Crushed close to her head was a black velvet hat in man's pork-pie style, from below which billowed fluffy white hair, like soap bubbles. Her wrinkled face was dark, hook-nosed, almost Hindu. Her eyes glittered, never wavering.

Oliver and the old woman stared at each other in silence,

a silence which Oliver found frightening, and which he broke at last with the blurted, foolish:

"I'm a thief. I want your money."

"I beg your pardon," Mrs. Vandle said. Her voice was a strong croak.

"I came for your money. Give me the key to the safe."

Still in a sitting position, the old woman glided smoothly several feet forward, when Oliver realized that her chair was of the wheeled type.

"Young man," she said, as calm as though this happened twenty times a day, "get out."

Oliver clenched his fists. "I'm serious."

"Get out."

"I'm not an amateur. Now give me the key or you'll get hurt."

"You are making me repeat myself, young man. Take that silly thing off your face and get out."

"I'm not going till I've got the money."

"Indeed?" Her large brown hands propelled the chair forward again, this time veering toward a table on which stood a telephone.

"The phone's out, lady," Oliver said. "We broke the connection downstairs."

Stopping her chair, Mrs. Vandle looked at him for a long minute. "I see."

"Morgan's not here and neither is Miss Farmer."

She nodded. "You have it all arranged, is that the idea?"

"Right. There's nothing you can do. Just give me the key."

Slowly the old woman reached up to her hat and from it drew out a long hatpin. She leveled the weapon at Oliver. "You want the key?" she said. "Try and get it."

Backstage at the Grand, two stage hands, an electrician, the producer, and three chorus girls, they were standing close to the wings and watching worriedly the performance of the Great Erik.

Out of the corner of his mouth, said one stage hand to the other, "He's making a real balls of this."

True. Erik could do nothing right.

Instead of gradually calming down, he had become more flustered, which caused new mistakes, which caused more fluster. His opening routine with playing cards had progressed so badly that he had given up and gone onto the next trick. He had managed to bring it off, but with such lack of co-ordination that no member of the audience was left in doubt as to how the trick was done. He got no applause. Several people walked out.

Erik's face was running in sweat. He was dazed and breathless, hardly able to merit his lack of control. And the harder he tried to enforce his skill, the less effect it had.

So much was his performance like the nightmares he used to have before important auditions, so unlike himself did he feel, that he began to hope he was dreaming. Perhaps soon he would wake up and go to meet Miranda.

He paused in looping a piece of rope on noting a bustle backstage. One of the Jonson Brothers, the comics, had come in with a flurry. The other people gathered around. Erik could hear excited whispering. One word stood out: *murder*.

Erik dropped the piece of rope.

Mrs. Vandle's maid still sat in the kitchen armchair, while Lefty Steel stood a yard away leaning his buttocks against a table. The woman now seemed less dumbfounded than before and less seized with horrified fascination of the gun. Bright color in her cheeks, she was looking around, from the revolver to the hideously flattened face to the open door.

Lefty's peculiar feeling was stronger than ever, and to him just as much a puzzle. He thought, though, that it might be due to the stocking mask. The mask was all wrong. It spoiled the scene. He had never yet seen one in a movie. Real gangsters didn't hide behind masks. Real gangsters weren't scared of showing their faces. Real gangsters weren't scared of anything—especially a stupid broad.

Out of his collar Lefty pulled the leg of the nylon and tugged upward. When it shot free he scrabbled the stocking into a ball and flung it contemptuously past the maid's head.

The woman flinched. She came even more alert. And, perhaps because of seeing revealed a youthful, pimply face, her alertness continued to grow.

Lefty scowled. This too was all wrong. The maid should be cowering, trembling, begging for mercy. All wrong. Nor did he feel less peculiar now that he was unmasked.

He waggled the revolver. "You know what this is, don't you?"

She frowned warily.

"It's a gun, that's what. It could give you the works dead easy. All I do is pull this trigger and you've had it."

The maid's spine stiffened until she was sitting erect on the chair edge. She said, "You oughter be careful. Someone might get hurt."

"That's for sure. Which someone is you. One false move —dead as a doornail. I kid you not."

"Now now."

"I've killed dozens in my time. Rubbed 'em right out. No fooling around with this boy, there ain't. Killed hundreds. You don't know who you're dealing with."

"Put it away," the woman said. "Don't be a silly boy."

Inside him, Lefty felt a mass of heat burst to life. It spread and burned as, open-mouthed with shocked rage, he stood up from the table. The heat reached his face and scorched it scarlet, reached his left arm and made it swing.

His fingers snapped across the woman's mouth.

She shot to her feet and swiped back, cracking him mightily on the ear.

Lefty fell.

The maid leaped for the door.

After a brief pause, Lefty jumped up. His face had changed. The redness had gone, he had a strange light in his eyes. He was now Lefty Steel, unskilled worker, only by a single cord. In the main he was every man reel or real who had ever packed a rod or pulled a job or rubbed out an enemy. He no longer had the peculiar feeling. He was exhilaratingly himself: Lefty Steel, gangster.

He all but laughed as he ran in pursuit of the maid.

In the large bedroom, Oliver Jet and Mrs. Vandle were enacting a weird tableau. Facing each other, a kick's length of space between, they were crouched forward in the poises of predators about to leap. Oliver's hands were raised and out, fingers spread. Mrs. Vandle stretched forward the hatpin weapon while keeping her other hand tautly, alertly on the chair's wheel.

Oliver had already tried circling the old woman. She proved too fast, too adept at swinging round her chair. With each try he brought himself dangerously close to the stinging point, which could easily be the killing point.

He had decided that a frontal attack was the only way. Rush in, deflect her thrust and grab at the fine chain that hung around her neck.

But the longer he delayed the more disorientated he became. The situation was hardly believable. The silent staring match, the dark, agile, evil-seeming old woman in her ridiculous hat, his own fear and tension and impossibly trembling legs.

And now, steeling himself finally for the attack, he held back in alarm at a clamor of pounding feet.

The following second, the situation would have been believable only to a lunatic.

In ran the maid screaming, "Mrs. Vandle! Mrs. Vandle!"

Mrs. Vandle began to scream, "Ellie! Ellie!"

The maid charged to Oliver. He pushed. She staggered away and fell, still screaming her employer's name.

Lefty Steel strode in. He took up a central position, spread his legs, waved his gun and started to shout in crazy hoodlumese, "Okay, you guys, this is it. The heat's on. You, sister, I'm gonna fill you full of lead."

"Mrs. Vandle!" the maid screamed.

"Run for the police!" screamed the old woman.

Lefty Steel yelled, "Don't worry, Ollie, I'm gonna fix these babes but good."

Dazed by the scene, hands pressed to his temples, Oliver suddenly realized that he too was shouting, though what the words were he was unable to tell.

With the knowledge of his shouting he broke it off. In

desperation he moved to act. He grabbed the maid, pulled and pushed her upright and out of the room, spun Lefty around and sent him rushing after and slammed the door on the racket.

The old woman chopped into silence.

Now, at once, Oliver saw the solution. He jumped to a heavy table and pushed it against the old woman's chair, forcing it back until she was sandwiched by a couch; next he swiftly blocked her in with armchairs.

Trapped, she glared, breathing heavily.

Oliver circled the couch. He leaned over. Mrs. Vandle tried twisting round, her weapon wavering high. He disarmed her with ease, flung the hatpin aside, and despite the old woman's evasions his hand found the neck chain. It came free with a snap—Mrs. Vandle crying out, Oliver mumbling, "Sorry."

Key in hand he ran to the safe.

At the head of the stairs Lefty Steel gave the maid a push. She went down head first and rolled, leaping and crashing like a drunken frog. Reaching the bottom she lay sprawled face up, groaning, sobbing, and making feeble movements.

Lefty stayed at the top. It felt good to be looking down. He spread his feet and sneered.

Onstage at the Grand Theatre, Erik was being as entertaining as disease. A good half of the audience had walked out. Backstage there had also been an exodus, but one spirited, excited. Now only the curtain hand remained.

Erik was drooping, exhausted with tension, worn out with worry. The act had been a total fiasco. He had failed to get himself under control and had made a mess of almost every trick.

Although ten minutes before time, he decided to bring the performance to a close. With great effort he produced what looked like six cigars from behind his eye patch, bowed and made a limp gesture to the remaining hand. The curtains came hurrying across.

One person in the audience clapped, three times, one

gave a sound of disgust and the orchestra burst with relief into a fast and unusually spirited *God Save the Queen.*

Erik closed his eyes. He opened them again suddenly to stop himself asking questions. He knew he would fall apart if he started to wonder what interpretations might be put on his dismal performance.

Tiredly he walked to the wings, where the stage hand was being joined by the musicians, who were grinning with eagerness. Erik listened to:

"Murder, is it?"

"Yeah, in the park, with everybody watching."

"A woman?"

"Yeah, a broad, a blonde. Shot six times, they say."

"Jesus."

"The body still there?"

"Hope so. I'm going now."

In bustled the group which had been there earlier. Erik, standing apart, noted dully that one of the chorus girls was crying. The two groups joined, there were more excited questions and answers.

"Still there?"

"Covered with a blanket."

"Who is she?"

"No one knows."

"What's wrong with May?"

"We heard someone say that the guy that done it was Dave Morgan."

"Say, I remember him. David Goliath."

"Lousy strong-man act."

"So what's wrong with May?"

"She's been going around with him."

Slowly, Erik turned his head and looked at the crying blonde.

Oliver Jet crouched before the open safe. He was aware only distantly of the obscene abuse being directed at him in a low strangled voice by Mrs. Vandle, who had finally given up the attempt to free her wheelchair from the blockade.

Although punched from his comparative calmness by the recent scene, Lefty's unmasked state and use of his name, Oliver had still been able on finding a stack of money to admit the emotion of, curiously enough, surprise.

He forgot it fast. Bringing out the pillowcase smuggled from the flat he began to stuff it with bundles of bills.

With the bolster three-quarters full he tied a knot in its neck; the remaining bundles he pushed inside the belly of his shirt. He got the passing impression that while the money would not amount to anywhere near the expected and advertised, there was yet a considerable sum.

He pulled out of the safe and scattered packets of letters and documents. Last he took out a small attaché case. It held jewelry, Nouveau Art pieces which his experienced eye knew to have value only in the gold. But every bit helped.

He rose, holding case and bolster, in his mask looking like a refugee from a holocaust. Mrs. Vandle began a last, violent attempt to free her chair. Oliver strode from the room, holding back the word of comfort he felt like offering.

He met Lefty at the head of the stairs. They went down together. At the bottom sat the maid, head in hands, sobbing quietly. Passing her they walked toward the door.

Midway there they stopped with a sudden backward wrench, like dogs reaching the ends of their tethers.

They had heard a squeal of brakes.

After exchanging a look, Oliver's frightened, Lefty's wondering, they ran into a dark front room and stared through the window.

By the gate stood a police car.

"No," said the man who was chalking his cue beside table one. "I don't know him."

"Lefty," Mr. Mortimer said anxiously, kneading shaky hands. "Young feller. Always around. You *must* know Lefty."

The swing doors burst inward and a man crashed into

117

the hall calling, "Murder! There's a murder in the park! Murder!"

Mr. Mortimer fainted.

"Cops," sneered Lefty. Oliver couldn't speak.

From the patrol car got two men, one in uniform. They began to walk along the drive.

Lefty gave a curious gasp-laugh. "We'll shoot it out, pal," he said. "We're not finished yet."

"Quiet."

"I hate lousy coppers. We'll kill the bastards. We'll—"

Oliver swung the younger man around and elbowed him back to where the maid sat. "Quiet," he hissed, addressing both. "Not a sound."

Lefty glared. "We've got to do something."

"It can't be for us. They're only checking."

"Checking what?"

"The address they found in Morgan's papers."

"Who?"

"They couldn't possibly know about us being here."

Feet scuffed to a stop outside. A knock sounded.

Lefty glowered at the door while Oliver—ignoring the maid, who seemed present only in body—glowered at Lefty, trying to will him to be still and be quiet. He was worried about the younger man's behavior, wondered if he were drunk or high on drugs, his manner was so strange, even manic.

The knock sounded again.

Lefty leaned toward the door, Oliver hissed warningly, the maid mumbled out her sobs, and from upstairs came:

"Ellie!"

Oliver shuddered. His control was growing thin. He told himself with unsteady sternness that the call from above was faint, could not be heard outside. Yet he wanted to run. He wanted to hide. It was intolerable, trying to divide his outsize apprehension four ways.

He was beginning to crack as he looked from Lefty to the maid to the stairhead to the door, when from outside came the sound of retreat.

Barely in control he ran down a passage beside the stairs. Lefty followed. They came to the back door, went out and ran across a lawn.

In the poolroom those watching were talking loudly and those playing were shooting quickly, all making up for time lost when everything had stopped out of respect for the passing of Mr. Mortimer's consciousness.

The proprietor was now free of his faint, slumped behind the counter in his chair, to which he had been carried, and insisting weakly to hoverers that he was fine, just fine, as people will when they feel like death.

The hoverers retreated, contenting themselves with peeping over the counter. Mr. Mortimer actually did begin to feel fine, at which point he remembered why he had fainted, and started to feel like death again.

He was swept by a wave of nausea. Fighting, grasping his head, he searched for hope and at once found it in the possibility that his remembrance was faulty.

He looked up at one of the peering faces. "What happened?"

"You passed out."

"Fainted," said another face. "Dropped flat on your back."

"Er, why?"

One face raised shrugging eyebrows, the other said, "Could be lots of reasons. Maybe we should get you a doctor."

"No, no, I'm fine. I think I was startled. Didn't somebody shout?"

"That's it. Now you've got it. You flaked out after Harry ran in to tell about the murder."

"Ah," Mr. Mortimer whispered.

"Somebody in the park. Thousands of people saw it."

"Lots of the guys have gone."

Mr. Mortimer stopped listening. He had the truth. He sank down in the seat. His nausea faded, his fear faded, feeling of any kind faded. He became empty with the nothingness of despair.

After a moment he raised his head again to look around. He tried to associate himself with what he saw. He could not. Already everything was strange, belonged to the past, with his life, which had just ended. Nor could he bring clearly to mind his house, his bicycle downstairs, his topcoat.

It was time to go. He rose tiredly and circled the counter. Someone asked, "All right now, boss?"

Mr. Mortimer moved away with a nod, and when the someone asked where he was going answered, "To the police."

Lefty Steel and Oliver Jet were creeping along the drive of the house next to Mrs. Vandle's; the older man, holding bolster and case, in a creep that was meant to be silent, the younger man in a creep that was meant to be sinister.

Seconds before, having crossed a fence at the foot of the Vandle property and crossed back over another, they had heard doors slam and a motor start up and then fade away. Now, breasting the house front, they saw what Oliver had hoped for and what Lefty could not have cared less about: the patrol car had gone.

"Come on," Oliver hissed. He strode toward the gate.

Lefty followed, frowning. He felt that a lot was amiss. Not in himself, being still a truer person than he had ever been. But in the circumstances. Things were not as they should be. The scene was all wrong. This hiding and running away and getting ordered about—wrong. And now the caper was as good as over.

He passed through the gateway behind Oliver.

Abruptly he became aware of the gun in his hand. He felt reassured. And with this feeling came the answer. He grinned. It was the one and only thing to do, the right thing, the thing everyone always did. He was surprised he hadn't thought of it before. It would put the scene straight.

He asked, "What's in the little suitcase?"

"Jewelry," Oliver threw back in a whisper. "Mostly junk."

"And the other's the dough?"

"Yes. Sshh. Come on." Oliver broke into a run to reach the break in the golf-course fence.

Lefty continued at the same pace, but his walk had turned into an exaggeration of his customary swagger. The cord connecting old Lefty to new was fraying.

He entered the speckled darkness of the cutting and came to the car. Oliver Jet, the case tucked under one arm, was pulling the stocking from his head. Lefty stood back, waiting, the grin on his face tight.

The stocking free and tossed aside, Oliver reached for the door handle.

Lefty barked, "Hold it!"

Oliver jerked round. "What?—Sshh!"

"Don't shush me, you son-of-a-bitch."

"Eh?"

"I'm through taking orders, buster."

Oliver Jet peered, leaning forward. "What's wrong with you, for Christ's sake?"

"This is the end of the line, that's all."

"End of the line?"

"That's right, pal. You're on the spot."

"What're you talking about?" the older man asked, his voice rising.

"I'm telling you. This is it. The showdown."

"You're sick. Too much excitement. Let's go."

Lefty laughed.

"Let's go," repeated Oliver and reached again for the door. He stopped again when Lefty called, singing out the words happily:

"Don't move. Don't make a move. One false move and you get a belly full of lead."

"Listen to me, son."

"Shut your goddamn mouth. I've listened enough. This is where I take over."

"Lefty!"

The younger man examined the name Lefty, found it acceptable, familiar, and said, "Yeah, that's me. Lefty. The toughest hood around."

Oliver Jet whispered, "Jesus."

"And this is it," Lefty said. "Curtains." He pointed the gun. "I'm taking that dough."

"You're what!"

"Drop the money."

What Oliver dropped was the attaché case, so that he could hug the bolster to him with both arms. He shrank back against the car, shaking his head.

"Come on," snarled Lefty. "Drop the dough."

"No."

"Okay, pal. I'm gonna let you have it. Right now." He cocked the revolver and, quickly, before there could be any change of mind on the other's part, which would have been too bad, aimed for his stomach and pulled the trigger.

The noise was like a small firecracker. Louder was the short cry from Oliver Jet. He loosed the pillowcase and fell, both hands flying to his left side.

"Told you, din't I?" Lefty said. He stepped forward and picked up the money, then, remembering, blew down the barrel of his revolver. Smiling, he went round to the driver's door. Now the scene was right.

Slowly along the residential street drove the patrol car, all its lights on, its radio giving out messages. The driver switched his gaze back and forth between the road and the gardens on his side. Another officer had his head out of the window; he scrutinized every patch of darkness, and before passing on gave the same attention to the bush behind which Dave Morgan was hiding.

Morgan had been regretting his actions in the park, hitting the policeman and running away. He told himself it had been the height of stupidity. But everything had been so crazy, scary. Miranda there jabbering nonsense and then being shot, seeing that familiar face, finally being pushed around by a cop and asked about the gun. Everyone seemed to take it for granted that *he* had killed Miranda. It was all mad crazy.

The sensible thing to do, he thought, was go to the police station and say, Look I'm sorry for hitting that officer, I panicked. Which was true. True and perfectly natural.

Morgan saw the roadway brighten. Headlights. The patrol car was coming back. He stood up. In a message on the car's radio he heard a name which made him drop flat again. The message was repeated:

"*Car Four, Car Four. Robbery at the home of Mrs. Vandle, Vandle, 28 East Park Boulevarde, 28 East . . .*"

The patrol car went on by.

Dave Morgan sagged with astonishment. Robbery at the home of Mrs. Vandle, he thought. No, it couldn't be. This was too much. Was he going mad? No, but something was mad, or very clever. This all tied in somehow with Miranda, with—

Morgan gasped as he put a name to the face of the woman whom he now knew was no woman. Erik. The Great Erik. Everything fell into place: Erik being called a cuckold, the telephone call supposedly from John Constance of *Spotlight*, Miranda talking nonsense and looking, he now recalled, as puzzled as he must have looked, Erik in disguise, the murder, himself standing there like a patsy, the robbery going on at the same time, Erik's association with the crooked Oliver Jet, Erik's persistence in trying to get friendly, Erik's talk of money. It all fell into place.

How they expected to get away with it he didn't know. What he did know was that they had tried to hang on him a murder rap while stealing his bread. It was the second he minded most—murder would never stick. The money was his, he had spent months on his plan, anyone who took that bread out of his mouth was a dead man.

Morgan got up and stepped cautiously to the sidewalk.

Dressed for the street, haphazardly, a hat perched at the wrong angle, one button on his coat incorrectly fastened, Erik switched off the dressing-room light and stepped out onto the catwalk.

He paused. He listened to the silence of the theater, felt its emptiness. Below, a single naked bulb lit the backstage area starkly. He didn't like the desertion. Normally he found it intriguing and romantic. Now it seemed wrong, almost menacing.

Nerves, he told himself; tension. There was nothing to worry about. Everything was going to be all right. So he had killed Miranda instead of Morgan. Either way it worked out the same. Morgan couldn't have recognized him, no one could place him near the park. All he had to do was burn the red coat and take the gun to the park and leave it, throw it in the trees, which is what he should have done before. Everything was fine. Not for a moment did he believe that Morgan had been seeing another girl and not Miranda. She was going to let herself be blackmailed, wasn't she?

All this Erik told himself while fighting the urge to fall down, scream with all his might and pound his heels on the floor.

He went down the metal stairway and over to the ramp. He was nearing the exit when he heard footsteps coming along the alley. It couldn't be anything dangerous, he thought as he stopped. He stood waiting.

The stage door opened. In came a uniformed policeman.

Erik cringed his head and shoulders. He ordered himself to run but his body continued to stand.

The policeman came up close. He glared. His voice was tough. "Erik? The Great Erik?"

Erik sagged. He was beaten. He nodded.

"Well?" snapped the policeman. "Where?"

"Huh?"

"Where do I find him?"

Erik realized with choking relief that he was not recognized—if, that is, the policeman knew what the Great Erik looked like—that he had again forgotten his eye patch.

He gestured. "Those stairs. Up there."

The policeman walked brusquely past.

Erik went on and passed outside. He was rumbled, he thought, fear following hard on the relief. They were looking for him. Morgan had recognized him or he had been seen by someone else or his putrid performance had been reported and interpreted correctly. He had to get away.

Erik broke into a run and sped down the alley.

The policeman strode up the stairway. His manner was tough because he was angry. The murder victim having been identified, he had been given the rotten job of breaking the death news to her fiancé.

Although it was small-town late now, on Lakeshore Drive the amusements were going full blast, and around the park, its gates closed, a crowd had gathered as news had spread of the murder, a rarity in Marlake. People hurried to and from the park or stood talking on corners.

Walking emptily on his way, Mr. Mortimer heard nothing, saw nothing. He felt neither physically nor spiritually —the cold without his coat, the ache in his head; remorse for what he had conspired to bring about, fear of the consequences. The past he had forgotten and his future of blankness he accepted. As for the present, he was propelled forward by disdainful conscience. The authorities had to be told the facts surrounding Dave Morgan's death.

His flat feet making smacks on the sidewalk, Mr. Mortimer went at a pace slow but firm, allowing no hindrance or distraction. He crossed a road in front of a car and was missed by inches; when on turning a corner he bumped into two drunken reelers he simply forged on between, heeding only as a distant rumble their volley of curses.

Gradually, into the void of his being crept a tiny voice, one of wonder. How was it possible that he at the staid and sensible age of fifty had allowed himself to be drawn into a crooked and ultimately murderous scheme? The answer was pride, ego. Not content with a small, fairly successful business and a modicum of position, he had fallen into the folly of wanting more, wanting to be bigger and better. The dream should have been kept in pleasant storage, not given concrete thought but merely brought out to pet like a kitten on quiet afternoons or shown in

confidence and wistfulness to close friends . . . close . . .
Mrs. Chaps.

Yes, he mused, Mrs. Chaps.

He turned a final corner and stopped. He was in a street
lined with tall houses. Only one was non-commercial. Odd
man out had a sign shining under the pillared portico
which stood atop the imposing steps from the sidewalk.
Marlake Police Station.

The windows blared light, though not invitingly, and
inside figures moved with an urgent briskness. At the curb
stood a patrol car, motor running, radio giving out snick-
ers and grunts.

Mr. Mortimer stayed on the corner. He was still thinking: Mrs. Chaps.

She ought to be told first, before anyone. The police end
was a cold formality, with Mrs. Chaps it was different.
She deserved a warm explanation (he thought without
warmth, still bleakly objective) and if the police came first
there might never be another chance.

He turned away.

It was quiet in the suburban street but to Erik the night
was full of sound. The pounding of his feet, the thudding
of his heart, the murmur of fear tolling *get away, get
away* and the voice of his mind working out the plan for
his safety.

It was too late to do anything about clues or evidence,
there was no point now in burning the red coat or leaving
the gun in the park; safety meant escape. He couldn't take
his car because they'd have a description and the number
and in any case they'd be stopping all cars. On foot was
the best way. He would go across fields, stay away from
roads and houses. He would get into the States and go to a
large town well away from the line and get an apartment
in a building that had hundreds of other residents.

Erik slowed to a walk. He thought there was only one
thing wrong with his plan—money. He had hardly anything
in his pocket and he daren't go to his room, where he had

126

over two hundred dollars. In any event, what was two hundred dollars?

Now, only now, did Erik recall the robbery. He wondered why he hadn't thought of it before. He supposed he must be in something like a state of shock. Imagine forgetting a fortune; or forty per cent of one; or all of one.

Erik stopped. He weighed his chances of being picked up if he went back downtown. He thought the risk worthwhile. He might not even be recognized. And anyway, he had the gun.

He turned and began to walk briskly.

Along Lakeshore Drive the amusements, in the process of being closed for the night, were crawling with people who wished to drink the gritty glamour's last dregs, drunks with no money left, couples who had had enough of each other and singles hopeful of a pick-up so that the evening could be ended with at least the traditional fumble on the beach.

A car drove by slowly. On the front passenger seat lay a bulging pillowcase; on the pillowcase lay a revolver. Behind the wheel sat Lefty Steel, smoking a dangled cigarette, one arm resting on the seat back, hand close to the gun.

Lefty had driven along the lakefront twice. Now he didn't know where to go next. Despite his insouciant pose, Lefty was puzzled. He felt at a loss. He didn't know where to go or what to do. It was as if he had an important date yet had forgotten the details. Important—he felt that strongly. His destiny lay waiting for him somewhere.

For the bolster of money he had not a single thought.

He shook his head. Sitting up straight, putting both hands on the wheel, he turned off the lakefront into narrow streets, where he continued to drive slowly, looking, thinking.

After going by a hoarding which advertised an instant coffee, Lefty sat a little straighter. New Lefty's shred of connection with Old Lefty had trembled as it received and passed on a message: go to Ed's Cafe, where the guys hang out: be seen.

While not so sure about this, Lefty moved to obey.

Picking up speed he drove past the gaunt-faced railroad depot, along beside a wooden wall which hid the track and stopped where the wall ended, in front of a cafe small and dismally lighted. In the window a juke box displayed its guts. Beyond, two men stood one on either side of the counter.

Lefty holstered his gun, climbed from the car and swaggered into Ed's Cafe. That the two men were familiar to him he found vaguely surprising.

He was ignored by Ed and by the customer—a plainclothes detective who lounged around town in the mistaken belief that no one knew him to be a detective in plain clothes.

Leaning on the counter, facing the others, Lefty put a hand in his pants pocket so that his jacket was pulled aside to show the holster's chest cord.

The men talked on. Subject, the murder of Miranda the Fabulous Contortionist. Plainclothes made statements which were actually questions and Ed pretended to be unaware of it.

Lefty thought that if only they knew *he* was the killer, that *he* had blasted the woman to hell in the park. Jerks!

He changed his hand from pocket to hip, revealing the handle of his gun.

The men went on talking, even when Lefty cleared his throat. He was tempted to tell them who had rubbed out that broad. That would shake the lousy copper a bit. Except he didn't feel that this was it, the thing he was looking for.

At last Ed turned to ask, "Something for you?"

"No," said Lefty. He sneered at the detective, swaggered outside and got in the car. Driving on, he wondered, now what?

Old Lefty supplied the answer. *Go to the poolhall; be seen.*

Two minutes later he stopped the car in Waterloo

Street. Half a minute more and he was pushing through the swing doors. Hands on hips, jacket bunched behind, he strolled between the tables, only two of which were now in use. Back of the counter stood a stranger.

Lefty asked, "Where's . . . ?" He wasn't sure of the name.

"Mr. Mortimer?"

"Yeah."

"Gone. I think he's sick."

"Gone where?"

"To the police. That's what he said. I think he's sick."

Lefty turned away, dropped his hands and marched to the doors. Now he knew what he had to do. This was it.

The cutting which ran into the golf course's frill of trees was silent and still. The birds were at rest, no breeze rustled the leaves. The only movement, and that infinitesimal, was the rising of the flattened grass on a set of tire tracks which ran beside the prone figure of a man.

Oliver Jet had lain for what seemed like hours entirely immobile, staring at the shadowy trees, senses tuned to his side, which felt hot and wet.

The pain had been fierce at first, cruel, worse than any pain he had ever experienced, making him convinced that he was dying; now it had grown milder and he had lost his awe of death. And so, at last, he decided to make an experimental move.

Slowly, eyes held tight as if he were listening, he pressed his palms on the grass and eased himself up. Nothing bad happened. He came into a sitting position. All seemed as before; the pain remained bearable.

He slipped a hand inside his shirt and ventured close to the wound. It was still bleeding, soaking the wads of bills and his clothes. The bullet, he surmised, had shattered a rib, whose splinters had helped enlarge the surface damage. With attention he would be fine. In fact he felt not unfine at the moment, apart from the pain and a certain lightheadedness, for his spirits were higher than they had been all evening.

He was no longer frightened or worried. The job was over. Next to failure or capture, the worse that could have happened had happened—shot by his suddenly deranged partner. The wound seemed fairly superficial and when the bleeding stopped would be harmless. He had come through the robbery well, keeping his nerve in a way which made him proud. He still had some money and Pel was waiting. Things looked good.

He ignored thoughts of what must have taken place in the park, not wishing to endanger his morale's delicate balance.

Grating his teeth at the way his rib rubbed its broken ends together he got carefully up, when he saw that Lefty had not taken the jewelry. He endured the added pain of stooping in order to pick up the attaché case.

Wiping off the sweat which felt cold between hot hand and hot brow he began to walk, each step a studied movement. He found that although the pain in his side increased considerably, sharpening his breathing, and felt but didn't want to make sure that the bleeding also increased, he was able to move without too great a discomfort. And move he must. He had to get home to Pel.

Near the edge of the trees he stopped. Along and across the street Mrs. Vandle's house blazed with light, as did the house next door. Outside stood three cars, two bearing police signs.

Oliver turned back. He reached the carpetish links and went along on the inner side of the trees.

He assumed that the neighbors had been roused to call the police. The hunt was on in full. Not that he was overly concerned. On foot he felt safer than in a car; who would think of the robbers walking? And as for long-term escape: he had left no prints and no facial image. The only danger lay in the police finding a connection through Erik, or in mad Lefty being caught and confessing, or in Mrs. Vandle and maid recalling *Ollie* being shouted.

But that was long-term. By then he could be hundreds of miles away, living under a different name. Nothing could be simpler. If only he got home quickly.

130

Fast movement, however, was out of the question. Already he was going at a slower pace than when he had started. While the pain was no greater than before, he knew now for certain that the action of his legs worked like a pump on his wound, sending out the blood in a steady stream. The hip of his trousers was soaked and he could feel the wetness moving down his leg. Also weighing against speed were a growing tiredness and the fact that his head felt lighter than ever, like a mild inebriation.

He stopped to rest. Almost at once he was on the move again, gasping, tread that of the blind on strange ground, body slanted over the pain, hand pressed tight to his wound.

The crowd that moved thickly among the amusements, closed or closing, was as interested in murder as the crowd around Marlake Park, or so it seemed to Erik, who had been through the latter crowd and was now circulating among the former. He heard:

"They say there's been three killings."

"Miranda, you know, the singer."

"They're looking for some guy called Morgan."

"There's been a robbery too and a gas station held up."

"I've heard it's a gang from Montreal."

"She was shot once in the back of the head. Biggest mess you ever saw."

"They got away with a fortune."

"Greg saw the killer. He touched him. I know Greg real well."

"Vandle. Old rich bitch. Took her for two hundred thousand dollars."

Erik, walking with lowered head, rubbed his tongue along the backs of his teeth at every mention of Mrs. Vandle's money. The robbery had been a success. He had heard mentioned amounts ranging from fifty thousand to three hundred thousand, which must certainly mean that the sum was substantial. Even the lowest figure would be a small fortune. Unsplit.

Erik pressed his bicep against the comforting hardness in his pocket. He told himself he was going to be golden, once he found Oliver Jet or Lefty Steel.

He had visited the poolroom, only to find it being closed by one of the regulars, whom he couldn't approach because he was known to the man. As Erik didn't know where Mr. Mortimer lived, he could do nothing else at that corner of the partnership.

There had been no answer to his knock at Lefty's house.

The doughnut shop door had been open. Inside he had called up the stairs. Above had appeared a man whose statement—that Oliver was not in—Erik had believed; there had been something about the man, his manner, his tone.

All three unavailable? Collusion? Erik chewed on this ugly thought as he worked his way through the people, bumping and being bumped.

One man he knocked against gave him a vicious, searching glance. Forgetting the possible treachery of his partners, Erik, not for the first time, had to reassure himself that what he was doing was right, that he was safer in crowds, where the police would never expect him to be, than creeping along quiet streets or hiding in doorways.

He went on, heart hardened against the laughter and funny hats, his ears straining for more titillating remarks about the money. He was having considerable success in avoiding thoughts of Miranda.

"Half a million bucks," a voice said. "Not a cent less."

Erik stopped to listen. The voice, which came from within a circle of people, went on to tell how it knew for a fact that Mrs. Vandle, who was a personal friend, always kept five hundred thousand dollars in her safe. She didn't trust banks. She also had a leather bag full of diamonds.

When another voice took over to repeat what it had been told about the holdups at three gas stations, Erik made to move on.

He glanced at another man, not of the circle, who was listening as well, a big man wearing a carnival hat with a wide floppy brim and a silly slogan.

Erik glanced, looked away, looked back with a snap.

Though only part of the face was showing beneath the hatbrim, he could see that it was the face of Dave Morgan.

Erik took a step back, at which moment the strong man looked around and saw him.

They both stared. Then Erik swung about and dashed through the crowd. At once he was bumping into people and the subject of hostile looks. He didn't care. He was petrified.

His shoulder was grasped at by a hand which a fast glance back told him belonged to Dave Morgan.

Wrenching free of the hand he twisted around a woman and sent her behind him with a hard push. He heard the woman yelp and Morgan grunt.

Now people all about were staring. But Erik still gave in to the greater, more immediate fear, and kept moving. He would have run had he been in the open.

He hit a man in a chest-on collision. The man was drunk. He threw his arms around Erik and said, "Steady, old buddy."

Before Erik could even begin to free himself his upper arms were taken in a strong grip and he heard above his head Morgan's voice say, "Sorry, pal, we're loaded too."

The drunk dropped his arms, smiled sloppily and fumbled in a pocket. "Let's have a lil drink."

"Gotta go," Morgan said.

Erik was turned away and moved on. He was amazed at the other's strength, at his own inability to resist.

"Look happy," Morgan hissed. "Laugh."

Erik produced an open-mouthed grin; only the fact of the gun in his pocket enabled him to manage that much. In any case, he told himself unsteadily, he was safe as long as they stayed in public.

Slowly they moved with the crowd. No one paid them any attention. Erik's grin stayed on, kept as a grimace for the pain in his upper arms.

When he was brought to a standstill by a pocket of gossipers, he heard softly from behind and above:

"You and me's gonna have a little talk, right?"

Erik said nothing.

"Sure we are. We're going someplace quiet and you're gonna tell me all about what happened tonight. Right? *Right?*"

"Yes," Erik said, gasping at the pain of the increased grip. "Yes."

"Sure you are, my dear good friend. Then you're gonna take me to the money. Right?"

"Yes."

"Sure. You'll be glad to. Then we'll go someplace else nice and quiet, and you know what?"

"What?"

"I'm gonna kill you, old pal of mine, that's what," Morgan said softly. "You know how?"

Erik shook his head. He was sweating with fear.

"I'm gonna break your neck. Your slender little dwarf's neck. I'm gonna turn your pin head to the side, slowly, slowly. Right at the end, when you're going mad with pain, there'll be a cute lil meaty crunch, and you'll be dead."

The blockage of people broke up. Erik was propelled forward. He carefully raised his lower right arm and eased its hand toward the inside pocket which held the gun. Only the tips of his fingers reached the butt. He could manage nothing more while his arm from shoulder to elbow was clamped to his side.

But soon, he thought. Sometime Morgan would have to let go, if only briefly.

The crowd had thinned. They were nearing the edge of the stretch of amusements.

Erik pushed back and forced a halt. He lacked the nerve to wait. He would have to try something now.

"What's up?" Morgan growled.

Erik swung his right leg forward, prayed for good marksmanship, and gave a powerful kick back. His heel found a bone.

Morgan spluttered out a cry. His fingers sprang loose.

Erik blundered forward, free.

The streets in the suburbs were quiet and deserted. Mr. Mortimer was alone as he plodded along, walking as if operated by a mindless machine. The houses repeated in division-measured doses the clap-clap of his feet.

His journey was nearly ended. He was glad. Used to his bicycle, too much walking on concrete hurt his soles. He told himself he deserved every ache he got.

Reaching Mrs. Chaps's house he knocked on the door. From beyond it he heard a rustle of movement followed by, nervously, "Who is it?"

"Mr. Mortimer."

"You sure?"

"Quite sure, yes."

The door opened. "Well, what a surprise," Mrs. Chaps said. "Come in."

He went into the hall. "I've got to talk to you."

His charwoman turned from closing the door. "Is it about the murder?"

He was glad the hallway was dim, that she couldn't see his face. "You know about it already?"

"Mary next door told me. What a thing in Marlake. It's not safe to be out. Decent people isn't safe. I near jumped out of my skin when you knocked. What a terrible thing. Murder!"

"It is a terrible thing, Mrs. Chaps. Despicable."

"People who'll do things like that." She shook her head.

"They're a menace to society. They should be put away."

"True."

"They should be put where they can't hurt others by trying to realize their stupid dreams."

"Yes, true, true."

Mr. Mortimer found himself saddened that he was being agreed with. He sneered mentally at his feelings.

Mrs. Chaps said, her voice shy, "I think I know why you came, Mr. Mortimer. You thought I needed protection, didn't you?"

"Well . . ."

"That was real sweet of you. Thoughtful. It's little things like that . . . You know."

"Yes."

In a firmer tone she went on, "And I guess it could

be pretty dangerous for any woman, till they catch this maniac that did it. I believe he shot her all to pieces, that poor girl in the park. Mary next door says . . ."

Mr. Mortimer stiffened. He stared. He broke into Mrs. Chaps's talk with, "What girl?"

"The girl that's been murdered. Just a kid, they say. Shot in the back. Beautiful too."

Mr. Mortimer continued to stare, now with horror. He realized what had happened. Erik had missed Morgan and killed an innocent bystander. A young girl. Beautiful too. And he himself shared the blame. How could he tell of this to Mrs. Chaps? He hadn't the courage. This was much worse than the planned death. They had committed a terrible wrong. He would have to go to the others and ask them to surrender themselves to the police. They would be arrested in time, but that wouldn't be right. They had to give themselves up.

"Is there something wrong, Mr. Mortimer?"

He shrugged helplessly. He was thinking of a beautiful young girl, dead because of greed.

"Oh," said Mrs. Chaps, her voice shy again. She looked down and gently cleared her throat. "If—er—you wanted to stay . . ."

Mr. Mortimer leaned forward and kissed her on the brow. He turned quickly and went out. At the gate he said in an undertone, "Good-bye, Mrs. Chaps."

The car moved slowly around Marlake Park, Lefty at the wheel. He was still looking for Mr. Mortimer.

After leaving the poolroom Lefty had gone to the police station. Through the glass doors he could see a lot of activity but nothing of the man he wanted. The fragment remaining of Old Lefty had urged New Lefty to make a telephone call. He called the police and asked for Mr. Mortimer. He knew the name well. He had been repeating it to himself.

"No one here by that name," the voice had said.

"Mr. Mortimer from the poolhall."

"Don't know him. Good night."

Lefty had decided the only thing to do was keep driving around until he found the man he wanted, the man he had to rub out.

Driving around the park had been gratifying. Everyone looked at him. He had been around six times. But now he was bored. The big scene, his moment, his thing, must be someplace else.

He swung out of the square which held the park, speeding up as he swung so that his tires would squeal. He drove along the lakefront, turned off into a side street, turned again into another.

He heard a shout. Slowing, he looked back. Running after him in the roadway was a man.

Lefty braked to a stop. The man opened the passenger door and leaned in breathlessly.

"Yeah?" asked Lefty, wondering where he had seen the man before.

"Where're the others?"

Lefty lifted one shoulder in a gangster shrug. "I dunno. Who're you anyways?"

Erik had been looking back to check that he had really given Dave Morgan the slip. He turned to look at the younger man. "What?"

"I asked who you are, Mac."

Erik saw there was something different about Lefty Steel. He had an odd twist to his face. Could he be sick, joking, acting?

"It's me—Erik."

Lefty shrugged again.

Erik looked down and saw a pillowcase. He put his hand on it as he said, "I look different without my eye patch."

Lefty frowned in concentration. There was something familiar about the man and about what he had said. Concentrating made Lefty's head ache. He put the task aside. Anyway, he was impatient to be off and find his scene.

Erik was excited. He felt sure the pillowcase held money. What else could those small crinkly bundles be?

He put his hand inside his coat and took hold of the automatic, saying:

"Who's that over there?"

The younger man looked away.

Quickly, Erik grabbed the pillowcase and backed off, stopping when he came up against the side of a parked car. He stood tense but confident, hand tight on the gun.

Lefty could see nothing. He turned, saw that the man had moved away, closed the door and drove on.

Oliver Jet felt as if he were drunk. His head was light, his vision blurred, his coordination poor and he was unable to keep a straight course as he shuffled across the pile of a putting green.

He knew, of course, that he was not drunk, knew that he was badly hurt. He had stopped pretending he would be as good as new with a rest and a drink and a piece of sticking plaster. His wound was still seeping out blood; his leg and its covering of material were soaked. All he could do was keep a hand on and bend over the wound, which seemed to ease the pain.

Every step made him more tired. The attaché case of jewelry, a weight of no more than five pounds, had grown into a barely tolerable burden. He would have stopped and put the case inside his shirt with the cash except that he couldn't stand the thought of how much effort the job would entail.

He dragged on, reached the knife-clean edge of the green and entered a belt of trees. He came alert to possible danger as the trees thinned and he saw beyond a hardtop road.

The open area was a clash of shadows, light coming from left and right. It was silent, eerie. Oliver had a sensation of unreality.

He peered out into the open. The road was lined neatly with turf, obviously not a public highway. To the right, a hundred yards off, stood a pair of tall iron gates, their pillars topped with lights; at a similar distance to the left sprawled a low building which was floodlit.

Clubhouse, Oliver told himself. He stepped onto the road and made toward the gates.

Abruptly, startling him to a gasping halt, he was enveloped in light from directly ahead. The beam moved, wavered, and he saw that it came from a flashlight held by an approaching man.

"Don't move there," he heard.

Lifting the wound-soothing hand to shield his eyes from the glare he thought: Stay calm, play it cool, this may not be the end, get the talent out and use it as it's never been used before.

The man was close now. Oliver said, his voice pitched between amusement and pique, "Are you trying to blind me?"

The glare lowered. The man came to a stop. He was in uniform. "Who the hell are you?" he asked.

Oliver returned his hand to his wound. "I might ask the same question of you."

"Me? I'm the night guard here."

"Of course."

"Don't you know this is private property?"

As if he hadn't heard, Oliver said, "Damned dog, it got away and I hurt myself."

"Huh?"

"My dog, a young pup, I took it for a walk and it got off the leash and over onto the links. I chased it and fell down. I think I hurt myself pretty badly."

"You're not a member here," the man stated.

Oliver shook his head briefly, impatiently. "That dog, I'll give a twenty dollar reward to anyone who finds it." He went on to describe in detail an imaginary dog, showing that his concern lay there, not in the fact of being a trespasser.

"Hear about the robbery?" the guard asked. His eyes seemed to be directed at the attaché case.

"Robbery is a widespread disease."

"This one happened just up the road. A pretty big haul, I hear. They're looking for the guys now."

"These crooks can get in anywhere. Myself I never take

chances. When I left the hotel to walk the dog I took my valuables with me. I always do."

"You got money?"

"Papers. But a smart thief would know they'd be worth a lot to a rival firm. I'm in electronics. Wilson Beams."

"Oh yeah? You work for Wilson's?"

Oliver gave a mildly embarrassed laugh. "Sometimes. I'm Edward Wilson."

"Ah," the man said. "Ah."

The other's tone gave nothing away. Oliver said, "Now, officer, if you could call a cab for me I'd be much obliged. I'd better get a doctor to look at my side. I think I've cracked a couple of ribs."

"Tell you what, Mr. Wilson, I'll drive you myself."

Five minutes later Oliver was in a car speeding toward the downtown area, listening dully to the guard's assurances that he would have no trouble in finding the dog.

Oliver slumped low on the seat, his head back and eyes closed. The effort of putting up a façade for the security man back at the golf course had drained him of his small store of energy, and while waiting for the car to come he had fought to keep his swaying body erect. He knew it was possible that the guard had not been taken in; their destination could be the police station. But he was almost beyond caring. He was more concerned with his pain and the flowing blood.

The car stopped. Oliver opened his eyes, raised his head with a drunken lurch. They were parked by the marquee of a hotel.

"Here we are. The New Flag, you said?"

"Yes."

The guard got out, circled to and opened the passenger door. "Give you a hand in, Mr. Wilson."

Oliver sat up. "Look, I'd prefer it if you could please go in and tell the desk clerk I'm here. He knows me. I don't like to keep you from your work."

"Check." The guard left and went inside the hotel.

Oliver moved fast. He thrust himself out of the car and set off to run. The pain shrieked up to cover every part of his body. He was unable to stop himself from crying out. A passing couple stopped to stare. Oliver plunged on at a broken stagger, face twisted, his arms out for balance.

He came to a narrow break between buildings, stumbled in and collapsed to the ground.

From behind the house's curtained windows seeped the deep drone of a TV set and enough light to reach the nearby shrubbery. There knelt the Great Erik. Before him were several untidy piles of money. He was counting.

When Lefty Steel had disregarded the loss of the pillow-case, Erik had thought with a vast drop of hope that his assumption about the money was wrong. A glance inside the bolster had made him smile—and wonder at the pimply young man's odd behavior. Erik had eagerly looked for a quiet place to assess his catch.

His counting was finished. Give or take a hundred, the money came to twelve thousand dollars. Erik sat back on his heels. If that was Lefty's share, he mused, a twenty-per-cent cut, that must mean that the total was sixty thousand. By agreement, he was entitled to twenty-four thousand, so he needed another twelve. At least.

He began to put the money in his pockets, planning what he would do when he found Oliver Jet.

Mr. Mortimer had left the outer suburbs behind. He was drawing close to the town center. He walked with purpose, still bent on getting the others to go with him to the police and confess. That was the first step in the direction of atonement, if it could ever be reached in full.

Mr. Mortimer shuddered with horror at the thought of the tragedy he and his partners had brought about. He told himself he should have known the scheme would come to a bad end. It had been madness. How could he have ever let his foolish dreams, his courting of the impossible, get out of hand? 50 Tables 50. Madness.

At a noise from behind, Mr. Mortimer turned to look back. Out of a house was coming a policeman, a lunch pail under his arm.

Mr. Mortimer stopped. He was unsurprised. Somehow he had been expecting a development like this. But should he fall in with fate or see the others first? As the policeman approached, changing from a stroll to an alert stalk on seeing the night walker, Mr. Mortimer decided there was no reason why he couldn't do both.

He said, when the other man drew level, "Officer, I have a statement to make."

The policeman, bulky, broken-nosed, eyed him carefully. "Oh, have you now?"

"I have."

"Had a drop too much, it looks like."

"I have a statement to make about the robbery and the murder."

Visibly becoming more alert still, the policeman asked, "What do you know about that murder?"

"Everything. After I've gone to see some friends for a minute I'll go with you to the station and tell the whole story."

"What kind of a gun was it?"

"German, I believe he said."

The policeman drew himself up. "Say, maybe you do know what you're talking about."

"Of course I do," Mr. Mortimer snapped.

Clearing his throat, stepping closer, the policeman asked, "Er, who did the shooting, sir?"

"That's enough questions. First I've got to see my friends. Come along."

Mr. Mortimer made the cross the road. His arm was grabbed by the policeman, who said, "Hold it hold it. Where d'you think you're going?"

"I've just told you."

"This way, sir. The station's this way."

Mr. Mortimer whipped his arm free. "First of all I'm going—"

"To the station." Again the policeman took up his hold, this time with a hard, experienced grip. "Let's not have any nonsense."

Mr. Mortimer was suddenly furious. Trying to wrench

away he shouted, "Let go, you fool!" He continued to shout and struggle as the officer began to move him along. The lunch pail dropped with a clatter.

House lights came on. A nearby door opened far enough to reveal a slice of face, to which the policeman called, "Phone the police. Emergency."

"No phone," said a voice, and the door slammed shut.

"Get off!" shouted Mr. Mortimer.

He choked off another shout to gag with pain as his arm was twisted behind and pushed up in a hammerlock.

"That's better," the officer said. "If you come along quiet you won't get hurt. Try anything, and you'll be sorry. Okay?"

Mr. Mortimer took deep, angry breaths. "All I want to do," he said evenly, "is see my friends for a minute."

"Sure, sure. After we've had a little talk with the CID boys."

One behind the other they went along the street, Mr. Mortimer forced to keep moving to ease the pressure on his shoulder. He mumbled to himself furiously. This is not what he had wanted at all.

A car cruised slowly by. The policeman shouted. The car went past, and as it did Mr. Mortimer noted vaguely how like Lefty Steel was the driver.

"Okay now," the policeman said, after throwing the car a curse, "would you mind telling me your name."

"I have nothing to say."

"But you'll make a statement at the station, won't you? The murder and everything?"

"No."

"You said you would. You said you knew all about it."

"I do. But I've changed my mind. I'm not saying anything till I've talked to my friends."

"Have they anything to do with the shooting?"

"I'm not opening my mouth."

"Look, I'll tell you what, when we get to the station I'll let you call your friends. First, before anything else."

"You will?"

"Word of honor," the policeman said. "Sir."

Mr. Mortimer mused that perhaps it was better like this. If he took the officer with him to see his partners they would have no choice in the matter, he would be giving them away. What he wanted was for them to come in of their own free will.

"Okay?" the policeman asked.

"Very well."

"That's the way. Good man."

Mr. Mortimer was alarmed to find that his emptiness was going, that he was beginning to feel again. Being called *good man* made his throat tighten. He was not good. He was a murderer. Yes, but only incidentally. He hadn't fired the gun. He had been blinded by ambition. There were . . .

He was, he realized, starting to make excuses. Did the return of feeling mean that he was going to try to avoid the issue? That was wrong. And Mrs. Chaps wouldn't like it.

Hastily he said, "My name's Mortimer, of the poolhall, Waterloo Street, and my accomplices are Lefty Steel and Oliver Jet and the Great Erik, and we got the robbery idea a few weeks ago. Are you listening?"

"Wait a minute, Mr. Mortimer. Don't go so fast. Give me the names again, please, with addresses."

After repeating the names of the others and adding where they could be found, Mr. Mortimer went on with the story of the Vandle robbery plan, and how death had crept in. Relaxing his grip, the policeman listened with care, on occasion putting a question. They marched almost shoulder to shoulder.

The story's end had yet to be reached by the time they came into the street which held the police station, when the policeman stopped the flow of words with a stern:

"Here we are, Mortimer. Now you can tell your story to the CID. And a goddamn pretty one it is."

Mr. Mortimer nodded as they headed across the roadway. "Yes, we're all murderers, I'm afraid."

"Murderers, yes," the policeman said, tightening his grip

and placing his free hand on Mr. Mortimer's shoulder in the official, textbook hold. "And something more."

They began to climb the steps. "What?" asked the prisoner.

"Scum."

Which was the last thing Mr. Mortimer ever heard, for the sound of the pistol shot had not reached him before the bullet crashed through his temple. He died as he started to fall.

With the explosion's noise in his ears and its smell in his nose, Lefty Steel eased back into the dark doorway fifty feet along from the police station. He posed, gun held at the ready, head curtly to the side so that one eye observed the scene.

Mr. Mortimer dropped to his knees. The policeman let go and stepped back, face open with surprise. He stood and watched as the older man fell over backward, tumbled slowly and erratically down the steps, rolled in spasms of impetus across the pavement and came to a stop on the curb.

Lefty also watched, and with such rapt attention that, forgetting his pose, he was drawn forward out of the shadow. Staring at the dramatically sprawled figure, he experienced a curious sensation, which even had it been given thought would not have been recognized for what it was: envy.

Lefty pouted, blinked, shrugged defensive shoulders.

The policeman came alive. He dashed to the curb, bent over Mr. Mortimer, straightened, looked swiftly all around, turned and ran up the steps and inside. A minute later all was confusion. Lefty sank reluctantly into the shadow.

People ran in and out, orders were shouted, someone called the policeman an idiot, another officer, gun drawn, went running down the street without giving Lefty a glance, a patrol car which drew up was sent speeding on its way again, the occupants likewise not looking at Lefty—making him sighingly mutter, "Dumb cops"—and Mr. Mortimer was carried untidily inside the building.

The street was suddenly and impossibly empty.

Lefty sagged against the door and returned his revolver to its holster. He felt let down. He still hadn't found what he was looking for. The big thing had not been here after all. The rub-out of the lousy squealer had been great, yet . . .

Now Lefty's expression changed. A word had come back to his mind, one that had been bandied around in hopeful tones during the final exchanges between the flurrying policemen. The word was *roadblock*.

His eyes gleamed and a smile began to form. Roadblock. Certainly. All the roads out of town would be guarded. Roadblock was *it*.

In the apartment above Waterloo Street's doughnut shop, the man and woman sat wide-eyed with waiting. Pel's hands constantly strayed, from the hem of her best skirt to the buttons of her new suede jacket, from her best earrings to the collar of her favorite blouse. Jonesy's hands, clenched into fists, were out of sight under arms folded bear-hug tight across the chest of his newest suit. By the door stood two suitcases.

Below, the shop door slammed.

Pel's hands made a frantic grab for each other, as if each were afraid of what the other might do. Jonesy performed a slow rise from his chair, tugged down his jacket and stepped stiffly to a position near the door.

There sounded thuds on the stairs; odd thuds, in twos, as though a cripple were climbing.

Pel rose to her feet while Jonesy ran an unsteady tongue over his lips.

The thudding stopped, the door swung open.

There stood Oliver Jet in a sag against the wall, breathing in a way that suggested great effort. His face, gray, the color of cement, was wretchedly drawn, the mouth grim, the eyes rimmed and shot with red. Not only were his clothes dirty, but his hair dangled, his shirt bulged and one leg looked wet, as though he had stepped into a deep puddle.

Neither onlooker spared the time to wonder at Oliver's rare lack of tidiness. Jonesy thought only with satisfaction that he looked shaken. Pel thought only that he looked old. In any event, the thoughts of both were mainly on a small attaché case.

Coming inside, seemingly reluctant to leave the wall's support, Oliver limped to a chair. He sat, wincing as his body settled. "Whisky," he said in a whisper.

Pel fetched a bottle, which with trembling fingers she uncorked and handed to her ex-lover. She turned away as his eyes caressed her with a disturbing exaggeration of devoted thanks. She didn't like the look and she didn't like his grayness.

Jonesy came forward to stand in front of the older man. Harshly he said, "Give me that case."

Oliver brought the bottle down from his mouth and mumbled, "Eh?"

"The case. Give it me."

Oliver looked puzzled. "What for?"

"Cos we're blowing, me and Pel. We want the money. Hand it across nice and quiet. You're no match for me so don't try anything."

Pel tensed up as Oliver's eyes sought hers, and then examined her clothes, and then skipped to the suitcases. He said, "No."

With Oliver distracted, Jonesy shot forward and snatched away the case. He opened it over at the table. After a low whistle of appreciation he said, "Jewelry. Christ, look at it."

Pel had moved to stand near the door. She averted her eyes from Oliver when he said weakly, "It isn't true. You're not going."

Jonesy laughed. He closed the case and tucked it under his arm. "It's true all right, Ollie boy. We've got the sugar and we're leaving. Me and Pel together."

Oliver said, "I've got money, Pel. Lots of money."

Jonesy laughed again, now in derision. "You've got nothing. You're finished. You can't work any more, only steal. And you always thought thieves were such a common lot, didn't you."

"Pel?" Oliver whispered.

"Oliver Jet, the big con man. Oh sure."

"Pel?"

"She's going with me. She don't want you. She'll tell you herself. You're old and finished, Ollie. Just old and finished."

"Shurrup!" Pel burst out, her back turned. "Let's leave, that's all."

"Okay," Jonesy said. He gave a mock salute. "So long, Ollie boy. Many thanks for the gift."

Pel picked up her suitcase. Jonesy got his and led the way out. Passing through the doorway Pel glanced back. Oliver was slumped in the chair, head to the side, mouth open, eyes closed. He looked dead.

"Come on," Jonesy said briskly as he trotted downstairs. "The quicker we get away the better. There's no telling how hot Ollie is."

Outside they had the street to themselves. They got in the panel truck, throwing their cases behind the seat. The jewelry Jonesy kept on his lap. He started the motor, slapped into gear and moved off, pulling the wheel around to circle away from the railroad tracks. With not enough room to make a full turn, instead of reversing he bounced up on the sidewalk.

As he bounced down, a patrol car swung into the street.

"Christ," Jonesy said. "Who they after?"

The next moment he knew. The police car, after surging forward, swerved to a stop in a side-on position across the center of the road. Out jumped three men.

"Oh Christ!" Jonesy gasped. He braked fast, leaped out with the attaché case in his hand, turned back and went racing along the street.

While Pel, being assisted forcibly from the van by a policeman, screamed the scream she had been fighting for some time, using it now to call on her lover to stop, stop, come back, another officer caught up with Jonesy and ran easily at his side and asked in a conversational tone, "Going someplace, buddy?"

Farther shoreward along Waterloo Street, beyond the railroad crossing, Dave Morgan stood crouchingly behind a parked car. He had discarded his carnival hat and felt naked.

Ten feet in front of him, kneeling beside the fence which separated house driveways, was the Greak Erik.

Morgan had been following Erik for the past five minutes. When first seeing the illusionist, slipping in and out of doorways, his impulse had been to charge in, take up where they had left off before. He had desisted because he thought there was a good chance of being led to the money.

He, and Erik, had watched fixedly the events at Waterloo Street's lakeshore end, and continued to watch as the woman, whose screaming had stopped, was pushed into a patrol car. Two more cars appeared, without sirens or commotion. The man who could be Oliver Jet—the distance was great, the lighting poor—and who carried an attaché case was shoved in beside the woman. They were driven off.

Two detectives entered a doughnut shop, another went to a house directly across the street, knocked and was admitted. The cars left, people from houses beside the railroad line returned indoors. Once more the street was quiet.

Dave Morgan rubbed his chin to help in thought. There was not much chance that all this action was unconnected with the robbery. That man must have been Jet, his case must have held the money. He was caught: the robbery had come unstuck.

Morgan's reasoning now seemed to be given the seal of fact. Turning, Erik began to creep back the way he had come; obviously the shop or the house had been his goal.

Morgan clenched his teeth in frustration and rage. He could already feel Erik's soft slim neck in his hands. He told himself this was going to be one of the most enjoyable things he had ever done.

Cautiously, Erik came out onto the sidewalk and approached. Morgan sank to a squat. The illusionist drew level, passed on.

Dave Morgan leaped up and out. Erik threw a fast, panicky glance back, then shot forward into a run. He jumped a low picket fence. Morgan followed. Neither man spoke.

Crossing a lawn, Erik tripped. He went sprawling. He fell to his hands and knees. Morgan flung himself on top of him but was carried onward, off again, by his impetus.

Three yards away in an undraped picture window sat a man reading a newspaper.

Erik rolled over, sat up and delved his hand into an inside pocket. Morgan was scrambling to his feet. He froze, in a low crouch, body kept from falling forward by one outstretched hand, when the other man pulled out a gun.

They stared at each other. Their labored breathing was the only sound.

Morgan shot a look at the picture window, at the same time giving a hiss of warning. Erik followed the look.

It was only a two-second distraction but Morgan had to take it. Another killing would be nothing to Erik.

Dave Morgan knew real fear as he flung aside the supporting arm and snapped straight his legs. The illusionist jerked round. Morgan landed on top of him. They both rolled over to lie side by side.

In the fast, fumbled struggle that followed, one pair of hands fought to get the gun while the other pair fought to aim it with certainty. The men holding their breath, the only sound now was body movement.

The scene in the picture window went calmly on.

Morgan got his hand on the automatic. To the accompaniment of a groan from its owner he wrenched it loose and tossed it aside. Fending off kicking feet and clawing hands he raised up, pushed Erik flat and sat on his chest.

Getting the thin arms under his knees was no problem. Now at last he was able to clasp the neck in his hands. He bent forward as he squeezed, watching the writhing features.

Erik made mouse-like squeaking sounds. His eyes glared. His legs flailed and his hands grabbed futilely at grass. Chuckling, Morgan squeezed on, gently increasing the pressure.

Erik began to mouth words. Was he begging for mercy? hopefully wondered Dave Morgan. No, it was one word, repeated. Morgan eased his grip.

"What?" he hissed.

"Money," Erik gasped. "Give you money."

"Where is it?"

"Pockets."

Releasing the throat Morgan patted Erik's clothing. He felt lumps. After moving his captive into a better position, holding him with one hand in an arm lock, he brought out the lumps, which were wads of bills. "How much is it?"

Erik sobbed, "Twelve thousand."

Grinning, Morgan put the money away. He shoved Erik down and returned to his former position. Wasting no time on gaining pleasure from the job, he began again on the strangulation.

Erik heaved and struggled. But only for a moment. Suddenly his body sagged. He had passed out.

At which point Dave Morgan realized the stupidity of what he was doing. There was no sense in killing the man. No sense or need. He could fix Erik good and be clean. He was clean now. He had committed no murder, he had committed no robbery. He was golden.

Morgan stood up. Retrieving the gun he stuffed it back in Erik's inner pocket. He looked around. The street was still deserted, the newspaper reader still absorbed. He lifted the lightweight illusionist, using the effort an average man would use with a child, put him over his shoulder and moved off.

In five minutes, walking quickly and boldly, having been seen only by a carload of singing drunks, he was approaching Marlake police station. Outside stood two cars, inside were people.

Morgan went to the center of the roadway, lowered Erik, gave him a judo chop to the side of the neck to prolong unconsciousness, let him fall in a heap and ran swiftly away.

Lefty Steel sped along in his uncle's car. He was no longer in doubt as to what he should do. Roadblock, that was it, his scene. He knew the routine well, was as familiar with it as the hotel maid finding the dead body bit. There would be flashing spotlights, barricades, crouching cops, machine guns. Big. The big time.

The biggest roadblock would be on the main highway, he knew. That was where he was headed. He had tried a minor road, turning back before reaching a junction where stood one patrol car, whose corny aloneness made him sneer.

The streets were dour with desertion, the houses mostly dark, the stores displaying their night lights, the traffic signals blinking yellow.

Lefty had a clear though unfortunately unobserved course along which to race his car. He gunned to seventy on the straight stretches and flung at corners on the wrong side of the road. He circled a traffic island in the reverse direction and when he came to a set of lights still working he slowed until red showed before speeding through.

From here it was two miles to countryside, to the last side road, to the logical place for a roadblock. Lefty became serious, holding his speed at a steady forty.

In front he could see a store whose tiny timid neon was snapping on and off. He stared at the sign. And he stared. His face twitched.

Gently, without fuss, the last shred of contact between the two Lefty Steels frayed through.

Smiling, he sighed.

He glanced beside him. The green glow from the dashboard played on the face of a man. The passenger was George Raft. Lefty glanced behind. On the rear seat sat a woman. She was Ida Lupino. Above the motor's murmur, faintly, as if from far away, could be heard pulsating music.

Lefty's eyes filled with tears. At last he had come home.

But this would never do. He blinked, shook his head and

brought out cigarettes, dropping one onto the lap of the man and tossing one over to the woman, who was looking through the rear window.

"Don't worry, kid," he said as he lit his cigarette, "we've shaken the tail. From here on it's going to be okay. This roadblock's nothing. We'll blast these hick cops to hell. Then it's us for the border. We'll hole up in Canada for a while, till the heat cools. Leave it to Lefty. Ever know me make a slip?"

"No," the man said. "Not you, Lefty."

"You're the greatest," the woman said, running a finger along the nape of his neck. "I could love you to death."

"Later," snapped Lefty, the boss. "Right now we got things to do. Check the artillery."

The man pulled a .45 from the waist of his trousers and snapped the safety off. From the floor to her knees the woman lifted a violin case and brought out of it a sub-machine gun.

"Okay," boss Lefty said. "We're all set. We'll show these crummy flatfeet a thing or two. They won't know what's hit 'em."

He put on speed to pass the last house. Ahead were two sets of headlights, unmoving, one on either side of the road. The lights were dipped.

Drawing closer, Lefty switched his own lights to the full. The other lights also flared up, while from between them appeared a police officer slowly waving a flash.

Lefty straddled the center of the road. He brought his car to a screeching, skidding halt with twenty yards separating the opposing lights. "Let's go," he snarled. Slamming out of the car he tossed away his cigarette and tugged out his gun.

He forgot about companions as he moved into the glare. The officer fast retreating on seeing the revolver, Lefty had the stage to himself. Into the very center he stalked, legs spread, gun jabbed forward. He was bathed in brilliant light.

He felt wonderful, wonderful, almost achingly great.

"Come on, you bastards!" he screamed, face distorted.

A voice called, "Put that gun down."

He laughed. "Scared, huh? I don't blame you. But I'm gonna give you first shot. That's the kinda guy I am."

"Put the gun down."

"Yellow sons of bitches!" he roared into the whiteness. "You're through, finished. No dumb cop's gonna fool with Lefty."

In a moment, he knew, they would shoot and a battle would start. They would blast away with their machine guns. They would spray him with lead, nearly cut him in two. He would go down shooting and throw the gun at them when it was empty. He would fall on his back and look at the stars and curse the cops with his dying breath. That's what he would do. He would fall on his back and have his long say.

But the end didn't work out like that. When Lefty fell, knocked unconscious by an officer who had circled round behind, he fell on his face and said nothing.

He heard voices. They echoed around him as though he were in a cavern. He began to remember. He remembered Dave Morgan, the money, being strangled. He wondered if he were dead.

The last mistiness floating from Erik's mind, he realized that he was alive, and in pain. His neck ached viciously. He further realized that he was lying on something hard and that beyond his closed eyelids there was a brightness of lights.

He decided he was in a hospital. Keeping his eyes closed he lay still and listened to the voices.

"That's not for publication. So watch it. Put that in your report and you get nothing else from me."

"Not important, Sarge. Do the Income Tax people come into this?"

"That's not our business. In any case, she's not saying how much is missing."

"Could I put an estimated two hundred thousand?"

"I don't care if you put two bits."

"You've really got nothing yet?"

154

"How many times do you guys have to be told? You wouldn't believe your own mothers."

"Come on, Sarge."

"Nothing. We got nothing. Only that crap jewelry. We've torn the flat apart and Lefty Steel's place and the poolroom. Nothing."

"Oliver Jet hasn't talked yet?"

"He's a pro. They never talk. All he'll keep saying is that he's not Oliver Jet, even though he knows we've sent his prints off. He keeps saying his name is, if you please, Jones."

Laughter: "Christ, what a brilliant imagination."

"Smith ain't fashionable any more."

"Maybe he isn't the guy you think. Wasn't Jet a con merchant?"

"He's our boy all right. His piece of candy told us. He's Oliver Jet, she said."

"So what's with the Greak Erik, star of stage, screen, and all points West?"

"We'll turn him up sooner or later. No one gets away on a stupid deal like this one."

Erik, numbed by surprise, stopped listening. He realized he was in the police station yet was not under arrest. He had not been recognized. How had he got here? But that could wait. What he had to do now was get out.

Erik opened his eyes and sat up, putting a hand to his brow in order to hide most of his face.

He was on a bench in a large room. Facing him over a counter was a fat, uniformed officer talking to two men in raincoats. There were three patrolmen huddled together at the end of the counter, while beyond it one officer sat typing and another was at a grumbling transmitter.

The fat policeman broke off and looked across. "You," he said sourly. "What happened with you?"

Erik's heart was beating fast. Watching through his fingers he said, "Dunno."

"We found you in the road outside. Think yourself goddamn lucky the cells are full. You got a record for public drunkenness?"

"No," Erik said. He understood why he had not been connected with the Great Erik. The police would not expect to find him on their doorstep.

"As if we didn't have enough to do tonight."

The two men in raincoats looked over. Erik recognized one of them as a reporter who had interviewed him at the start of the season.

"I'm not used to drink," Erik said thickly, covering more of his face. "I guess the night air finished me off."

"I could book you for this."

"I'm on vacation, officer."

"You tourists think you can do just what you goddamn like around here."

"Sorry."

The policeman nodded toward the door. "Take off."

Erik rose unsteadily. The reporter was watching him with a frown.

"And stay sober," the policeman growled.

Erik nodded, still keeping his hand to his face. He turned. The doors were four yards but looked forty yards away. Through the glass, the street waited, smiling.

Erik moved. He remembered with a coldness of fear which made him actually shudder that in his pocket was the gun, the murder weapon.

"Just a minute."

Erik stopped.

"Hey, just a minute."

Erik had to turn.

The fat officer said, "I'd better take your name and address."

The reporter was looking at him with slanted head of self-query. Erik said, "Whitson. Charles. Two-six-eight-four Organdy Street, Hamilton."

The policeman scribbled. He lifted his head and looked toward the door, everyone looked toward the door. From outside had come the sound of a stopping car.

Someone said, "This'll be the roadblock guys with Lefty Steel."

Erik's mouth opened in horror. He began to back toward

the outside sounds of slamming doors and approaching footsteps. Everyone in the room was looking past him. He had been forgotten.

The doors whined open. Shoes clattered on the linoleum. A man walked by. He was followed by a uniformed officer. Handcuffed to the officer was Lefty Steel.

Erik took another step backward.

Lefty glanced at him. He prolonged the glance into a look. He stopped, drawing the officer back.

Lefty's face was slack and white. There was dried blood on his ear. There was dirt on one cheek and on his clothes. His eyes were glazed, unblinking. He looked like a sleepwalker.

"What the hell's wrong with you?" grated the officer. The other men were watching closely.

Lefty's blankness of face changed. He frowned in concentration. Raising a hand he pointed limply toward Erik.

Erik was unable to move. He stared at the lips of the younger man, which looked as though they were trying to produce a word.

"Let's go," the officer snapped, tugging on the handcuffs.

"Leave him alone," someone said.

Erik stared, the lips moved, the room watched.

At last, with a twitch that seemed to take in his whole body, Lefty Steel found the word he had struggled for. He said, "Erik."

Erik broke apart. He gave up the hour-long battle for calm and sanity. Covering his face with both hands he flung himself down, kicked his feet on the floor and screamed, "I won't, I won't, I won't!"

In the deep, shadowy doorway of an office block knelt Oliver Jet. One hand was pressed to his wound, the other held a bottle of whisky. His eyes were closed. There was about him the odor of defeat.

Earlier, at the apartment, after Jonesy and Pel had left, he had gained the will to ignore his pain and his tragedy when hearing in the street the sounds of capture. Stagger-

157

ing to the door he had gone down the stairs in a bumpy slide, entered a back room and let himself out into an alley. He had stumbled on until, reaching the office block, he felt he could go no farther. He had gone into the entrance crawling.

Now he was past caring about escape. He was consumed by his aches. One, on the surface, was bearable. The other, inside, was not. Had he owned the necessary strength, he would have wept. As it was, he merely sat, slumped low, his mind fogged. He had given in.

Except . . .

Except that there was something . . .

Oliver roused himself enough to shakily lift the whisky bottle to his lips. He gulped down three mouthfuls.

Except that there was something he could do, should do. Something to restore the balance.

For a moment, as Oliver thought hard, his inner ache and the fog of his mind faded. What it was he wanted to do, however, he still couldn't see. It lay too deep. And then the moment of clarity had gone.

Move, said the voice within. You'll understand soon.

Stiffly, inch by inch, he pulled himself upright. To recover from the effort he paused, and in the pause swayed.

His head felt lighter than ever; it seemed to be floating above his body, keeping aloof from the torment. The ache in his side ground on. One shoe felt as though it were full of gooey mud; when he stepped forward he left a dark footprint with glistening edges.

He moved, each step a pain-won achievement, the wrench making his wound feel like a yawning jaw. At the front of the doorway, after a brief rest, he went out and moved up the street.

If he was dying, he thought, it was sad, because he would never be able to pay the rest of the money for the gun. Perhaps that was the worry that was driving him on.

Coming level with a beer parlor, getting a whiff of its smell, he realized he still held the whisky. Taking a gulp, he set the bottle down in the pub door.

Another moment of clarity came. He understood. Tired eyelids nodding in assent, he moved on.

He turned onto Lakeshore Drive. Complete desertion. Sighing with disappointment he went along beside the shrouded stalls. He peered into shadows and saw no one.

Past the amusements he came to a turning. He edged to the corner and put out an unsteadily searching hand to find the wall, found it and eased his body into a lean. He wanted to lie down. He wanted to rest a long time. It seemed impossible that he could remain standing. Yet he could. He had to.

There was the sound of a train shunting.

That's it, the voice within him urged. That's the place.

On he went, one supporting hand against the wall, head bowed to the pain. His heart pounded, his feet slurred, his shoe squelched and his breath struggled.

The surroundings were becoming indistinct: buildings and lampposts leaning, large lights fuzzing and small ones growing haloes, roadway and sidewalk blending in a gray ribbon with cambered sides.

By alternating blinks with stares he killed some of the indistinction; some; underfoot was the same. Or perhaps this was not due to vision, for he felt sure that the camber was real, that he was climbing. He forged ahead. Nothing must hold him back.

At last he arrived in front of Marlake's railroad depot. He passed into the hall. One ticket window was open but unmanned, a couple necked in a dim corner and three girls in hiking clothes slept on a bench. Oliver stared at the couple for a foggy minute before moving on.

The dead-end track stretched away to the right. Fifty yards along stood a hissing train and people. Near the people were two men in plainclothes who had to be detectives.

Oliver stopped.

Behind him he heard a squeal of brakes, a car door open and close, firm footsteps. He closed his eyes.

He opened them again when the footsteps went past. A police sergeant was striding by; he went to the two detectives and spoke; all three came walking back.

Not one of them looked aside as they passed within a yard of where Oliver stood swaying. He heard the car start, leave.

He made a supreme effort. He forced his body into a forward stagger. He scraped, stumbled, and weaved, his eyes on the waiting train and its attendant group of see-ers off, some with handkerchiefs at the ready.

Oliver went on, slowly now, his feet shuffling. The effort had brought him to the penultimate moment of collapse.

He reached his goal. Into his blurred vision appeared a porter, who gestured at the first of the train's doorways and beckoned quickly. "Just in time, chief. Hop in."

Dave Morgan, in cap, spectacles, padding and coat, watched the platform through the train window. He was almost fully relaxed. His plan had worked. Getting his disguise from the back of the Cadillac had been simple— the house in darkness—and the detectives here had looked at him without interest. To make everything cozy, a sergeant had just come to the pair and taken them off.

Lip-reading, Morgan had followed the exchange.

"It's okay, we've got the magician guy, Erik. That's the lot."

"And Morgan?"

"No, but we don't know if he fits into this."

Dave Morgan squeezed his shoulders inward with delight. He was golden. He was not so rich as he might have been, but he was clean and moneyed.

Now Morgan sat up straight. Outside, near a porter, had appeared no other than Oliver Jet. Was he not in on the caper after all?

Morgan watched tensely.

Oliver Jet reached the porter's side, passed him by, turned away from the train and went to the group of people. The porter shrugged, waved his arm. A whistle blew. The train gave a preliminary shudder. Oliver Jet, his face a terrible shade of gray, stopped in front of a woman, who looked at him worriedly.

The train began to move.

In the few seconds before the scene was gone, Dave Morgan saw Oliver Jet bring from inside his shirt a crumpled handful of bills, thrust them into the startled woman's hands and tell her earnestly, sadly, in aching confidence, "I'm Oliver Jet."